William H. Venable

Footprints of the Pioneers in the Ohio Valley

a centennial sketch

William H. Venable

Footprints of the Pioneers in the Ohio Valley
a centennial sketch

ISBN/EAN: 9783337252137

Printed in Europe, USA, Canada, Australia, Japan

Cover: Foto ©Andreas Hilbeck / pixelio.de

More available books at **www.hansebooks.com**

1788.   1888.

FOOTPRINTS

OF THE

PIONEERS

IN THE

OHIO VALLEY

A CENTENNIAL SKETCH.

BY

W. H. VENABLE LL D

CINCINNATI, O.
OHIO VALLEY PRESS, PUBLISHERS.
1888

TABLE OF CONTENTS.

List of Illustrations.

CHAPTER FIRST.

FRANCE AND ENGLAND IN THE WESTERN WORLD.

AMERICA'S QUADRI-CENTENNIAL.

"WESTWARD THE COURSE OF EMPIRE
TAKES ITS WAY;
The first four acts already past,
A fifth shall close the drama with
the day;
Time's noblest offspring is the
last."

Four centuries ago, lacking four years, counting from this present writing in 1888, Columbus discovered America. The world will celebrate the quadri-centennial of that great event in 1892. But the white foot did not get a firm hold on that part of the continent now mapped the United States until after many attempts and failures. When a hundred years had

elapsed, after Columbus first saw the border of the New
World, the only white settlement north of latitude
thirty degrees, in America, was a small colony of
Spaniards at Santa Fé, then within the province of
Mexico. If we consult the colonial records of census,
we learn that the sum total of the English-speaking
population of this country, only two hundred years
ago, was not one-tenth so numerous as that of Ohio in
the present year. The city of Chicago contains about
half as many people as the colonies contained at the
close of the French and Indian War.

It is now but twelve years since the people of the
United States commemorated the founding of the
Nation, by holding at Philadelphia a grand centennial
exposition celebrating the hundredth anniversary of
Independence Year—1776. In this year of our Lord,
1888, the citizens of Ohio and her neighbor States,
unite to celebrate, by several demonstrations in various localities, what may be not inappropriately called
the centennial anniversary of the birth of the great
Northwest.

The whole history of civilization in the United
States is known. We know why, when, and how men
of Europe came to the western continent; how they
made discoveries and fixed settlements; how the English colonies crowded out or swallowed up all other
nationalities, and founded powerful States; how these
States joined to cast off the rulership of Great Britain
and became a distinct nation—one great State comprising several smaller Commonwealths.

The history of the Republic, from its birth in 1776
to its present age of one hundred and twelve years, is
recorded in countless volumes. The life-story of America is complex, being the annals of many in one; the

career of each several State must be studied in order to understand the history of the Union; yet the great features of general progress may be traced without much difficulty. These great features should be familiar to every man and woman who lives a subject of our government. Teachers should teach and children learn how we came to have a Fourth of July; how the Nation born on the first Fourth of July grew strong and great; how it passed through several wars; how slavery existed in the land and how it ceased to exist; how the population spread from east to west, forcing the wild tribes from their hunting grounds and changing the wilderness into farms and towns; how the manner of living altered as the country became older; how the many streams of foreign migration have mixed and mingled in one vast ocean of loyal Americanism; how fortunate discoveries and useful inventions have added constantly to the wealth and convenience of the people; and how, to-day, millions of citizens enjoy the blessings won by the bravery, industry, patriotism and forethought of those who lived before our time.

THE YEAR 1888.

The year 1888, regarded as an anniversary, is of such interest, both special and general, that its celebration is an important event in the world's history. The Constitution of the United States was ratified just a century ago. The vast territory northwest of the Ohio River, now comprising five great States, was settled a hundred years ago within the limits of the present State of Ohio, which State, however, had no separate existence in 1788. Ohio being the eastern part of the general domain called the Northwestern Territory, was naturally the region first to be populated, and first to be organized under a State government. She was the first-born of the five sisters. This gives Ohio a peculiar distinction, and entitles her to special privileges in the year's rejoicings. Therefore her own citizens, and those of Indiana, Illinois, Michigan, and Wisconsin, combine to do honor to the representative Commonwealth, Ohio. Scarcely less is the interest which other and older neighboring States share in the memorable occasion. Pennsylvania, the Virginias, Kentucky, and Tennessee—all the States of the Ohio Valley—are united by ties commercial, social, and patriotic. The whole Nation sympathizes with this demonstration, as the body feels in its every member. North and South here coälesce, for, as has been said eloquently by William P. Cutler, a son of the founder of the Ohio Company, "Massachusetts and Virginia joined holy wedlock and Ohio was their first-born."

Discovery of the Great West.

The accurate and brilliant writings of Francis Parkman have familiarized readers of history with the romantic lives of Champlain, Marquette, and La Salle, whose daring footsteps led a host of missionaries and soldiers to New France, a name which once applied to a large portion of North America. Imagination plainly pictures the hardy adventurers of the seventeenth century, pushing their way westward, along the Great Lakes, now bearing their canoes on their shoulders, now launching in unknown waters, guided and assisted by the bronzed natives of the forest. Two centuries and a half ago Jean Nicollet, the French interpreter, who lived with the Indians and like an Indian, discovered the Wisconsin, and thought himself within three days' journey of the South Sea. La Salle discovered and navigated the Ohio River in 1669 or 1670; in 1679 La Salle built and launched "The Griffin," the first vessel that sailed the upper lakes, and in 1682 he floated down the great "Messipi."

Thus was the "Great West" discovered. The banner of France and Navarre ruled Louisiana, a region that spread from the Alleghanies to the Rocky Mountains, and stretched from the Lakes to the Gulf of Mexico.

The name Louisiana was given in honor of Louis the Fourteenth, the "Grand Monarch," who is remembered for having said: " I am the State."

The circumstances attending this discovery of the Beautiful River—*la belle riviere,* as the French named the Ohio—are enveloped in mystery. But that Robert Cavalier de La Salle is entitled to the glory of leading the first exploration to its banks, there can be no doubt. History accepts it as an established fact that early in July, 1669, this bold adventurer left Montreal at the head of an exploring party, and that he probably spent the winter of 1669-70 in the Ohio country between Lake Erie and the great stream which the Indians called "Ohio," "Oligheny-sipu," or "Meesch-zebe." Writers conjecture variously that he reached the Ohio by following down either the Muskingum, the Scioto, or the Big Miami. Having come to it by one or another of its tributaries, he floated upon its current, in a canoe, as far down as the falls, opposite where Louisville now is.

The French Government claimed and held jurisdiction over Louisiana, including, of course, the Ohio Valley, for ninety-three years. The State authorities at Paris, in their instructions to M. Du Quesne, in

1752, declared that "The Ohio, otherwise called the Beautiful River, and its tributaries, belong, indisputably, to France, by virtue of its discovery by the Sieur de La Salle, and of the trading posts the French had there since."

On the east side of the Alleghanies a rival standard was displayed—the menacing colors of St. George. Our girls and boys know from their school histories how and when the British Lion came to Virginia and to New England; how, having devoured the Dutch Colony as his prey, he pounced upon and finally swallowed his formidable rival New France.

Conquest of New France.

From the year 1534, when Cartier discovered the St. Lawrence, and laid claim to North America for France, the English nation, basing a prior right to the continent by virtue of Cabot's discoveries in 1497, contested the rival claim. A series of intercolonial wars, beginning in 1689 and closing in 1748, a period of fifty-nine years, led up to the final struggle between France and England for the possession of the interior. This struggle began when, in 1754, some French soldiers drove away a party of English who were building a fort at the head of the Ohio. The French completed the fort and named it Du Quesne. This precipitated the war which was not terminated until September, 1760, when the Marquis de Vaudreuil capitulated at Montreal, and surrendered New France to the British Crown. In 1763, France formally ceded to England her possessions lying east of the Mississippi, and to Spain the territories west of that river. Spain also ceded to England the whole of Florida. This treaty of 1763 secured to Great Britain all that portion of

North America lying east of the Mississippi, and from the Gulf of Mexico to the Arctic Ocean.

Great Britain held these possessions twenty years, or until the close of the Revolutionary War, 1783 when, by the Paris treaty of peace, British America, was limited to the territory north of the Great Lakes and the St. Lawrence, and the United States became owner of the larger section bounded by Canada, the Atlantic Ocean, the Gulf, and the Mississippi. The immense area north of the Ohio, then claimed by Virginia, was formed by that State into a territory called Illinois, which, in 1784, was ceded to the Federal Government, and was afterwards distinguished as the Northwestern Territory. The land west of the Mississippi River was ceded by Spain to France, and remained in possession of the latter country until April, 1803, when it was sold by Napoleon Bonaparte to the United States for the sum of $11,250,000.

THE OHIO LAND COMPANY OF VIRGINIA.

Long before the termination of the old French War, the English recognized the importance of getting permanent possession of the interior of the continent. Bancroft says: "To secure Ohio for the English world, Lawrence Washington, of Virginia, Augustus Washington, and their associates, proposed a colony beyond the Alleghanies. 'The country west of the great mountains is the center of the British dominions,' wrote Halifax and his colleagues, who were influenced with the hope of recovering it by some sort of occupation; and the favor of Henry Pelham, with the renewed assistance of the Board of Trade, obtained in March, 1749, the King's instructions to the Governor of Virginia, to grant to John Hanbury and his associates in Maryland

and Virginia five hundred thousand acres of land between the Monongahela and the Kanawha, or on the
northern margin of the Ohio. The company were to
pay no quit-rent for ten years, within seven years to
colonize at least one hundred families, to select immediately two-fifths of the territory, and at their own cost
to build and garrison a fort. Thomas Lee, President
of the Council of Virginia, and Robert Dinwiddie, a
native of Scotland, Surgeon-General for the Southern
Colonies, were shareholders."

The Ohio Land Company of Virginia was thus organized in 1748. Rewards were offered to hunters and
wood-wise scouts who should track the wilderness and
discover the most practicable routes.

In 1750 a path was discovered to the Ohio by Wil-
lis Creek (Cumberland), and traders carried goods to
that creek and there sold them. Christopher Gist, the
company's surveyor, made an expedition down the
Ohio, which La Salle had found and named eighty
years before. A French trading post had been erected
near the mouth of the Scioto, on the Ohio, before the
year 1740, about half a century earlier than the founding of Marietta. Gist carried the surveyor's chain to
within fifty miles of the Falls of the Ohio. He visited
various Indian tribes and villages, endeavoring to win
their allegiance to the English. Bancroft tells us that
he "gazed with rapture on the valley of the Great
Miami, 'the fairest meadows that ever can be.'"

It was under the auspices of the Ohio Company of
Virginia that the English began, in 1754, to erect the
first fort at the fork of the Ohio, where Pittsburgh now
stands. The French captured this fort and named it
Du Quesne. This precipitated the war which ended
in the conquest of New France.

MIGRATION TO THE WESTERN WILDERNESS.—SETTLEMENT OF KENTUCKY AND TENNESSEE.

After the French and Indian War (1760), English settlers began to occupy lands along the Great Lakes and the chain of lakes in Northern New York. They made way, also, through passes in the Appalachians and around the southern ranges, like water seeking

DANIEL BOONE.

the easiest channel, and came to rest in the valleys of the Cumberland, Tennessee, and Ohio. But the stream of pre-revolutionary migration was scant, and the war checked its feeble current for seven years.

As when the discovery of America is mentioned we immediately think of Columbus, so when the settlement of Kentucky is spoken of we recall Daniel Boone. The association is very helpful to memory. The student of history should always bear in mind the

2

true relation of events to the time when and the place where they occurred. The cause, progress, and outcome of occurrences can be understood only by conceiving historical characters and events in the order of sequence. It is useful, for example, to remember that, in the later battles of the Revolutionary War, especially in the fight at King's Mountain, many patriots volunteered from the back-woods of Kentucky and Tennessee. This fact makes the mind realize that a white population had colonized regions west of the mountains before the struggle for national independence had ended, and long before the Father of his Country became President. Boone made his first exploration in Kentucky in 1769; and before Jefferson penned the Declaration of Independence there were settlements on the Holston River, Tennessee, and at Harrodsburg, Boonesborough, and other stations in Kentucky. Once fairly started, so rapidly did the current of migration flow westward that by the year 1790 Kentucky had a population of seventy-three thousand, which, in 1800, had increased to two hundred and twenty thousand. In the single year 1784, four years before Ohio received her first colony at Marietta, thirty thousand people came to Kentucky from Virginia and North Carolina. They came, as the homely phrase is, "by Shanks' mare." They *walked* into the famous Hunting Grounds, so often baptized in blood, and bearing the sanguinary name "Caintuckee."

They filed into the magnificent valley of the Ohio, traveling through Cumberland Gap and along the famous route marked out by the original pioneers, and which is used to this day. The road was at first but a trace. No wheels rolled through the westwood until after the State Legislature, in 1795, took action to make a wagon road. The Filson Society, of Louisville, published, in 1886, an interesting book, by Thomas Speed, giving a history of the "Wilderness Road." The following quotation is from Mr. Speed's careful volume.

"The distance from Philadelphia to the interior of Kentucky, by way of Cumberland Gap, was nearly eight hundred miles. The line of travel was through Lancaster, Yorktown, and Abbottstown to the Potomac River, at Wadkin's Ferry; thence through Martinsburg and Winchester, up the Shenandoah Valley through Stanton, and following the great trough between the mountain ranges, it passed over the high ground known as the 'Divide;' there it left the waters which 'run toward sunrise,' and reached an important station at the waters of New River, which ran to the west. At that point, another road which led out from Richmond, through the central parts of Virginia, intersected or rather came into the one just described. Thus were brought together two tides of immigrants. Near the forks of the road stood Fort Chissel, a rude blockhouse, built in 1758, by Colonel Bird, immediately after the British and Americans captured Fort Du Quesne from the French, and called it Fort Pitt. Fort Chissel was intended as a menace to the Cherokee Indians; it was an outpost in the wilderness of the West, yet from the point where it stood to Cumberland Gap was nearly two hundred miles. "

In the year 1774, Boone walked from the Clinch River settlement to the Falls of the Ohio, following the Wilderness Road. The distance was eight hundred miles, and the journey consumed sixty-two days. Through the rocky defiles of Cumberland Gap, Boone, in 1775, conducted his own and five other families to fix the white man's habitation in the garden of the savage.

Through the same stony gateway, and along the same forest-hidden path, did General George Rogers Clark, the conqueror of the North-west, make his journey in 1775. By the old Wilderness Road came the Rev. Lewis Craig, conducting his congregation of Baptists from their home in Spottsylvania, Va., to find religious liberty in the free wilds of Kentucky. Tramp, tramp, tramp, moved men, women and children, over the mountains from Carolina and the Old Dominion, to establish a new dominion by dispersing the buffalo, the catamount and the beaver. Literally they stood upon their own feet. The law of the survival of the fittest was never put to a severer test. Strong must the constitution have been of him and her who walked

> " Over stock, over stone,
>   Through bush, through briar,"

for hundreds of miles, in all weather, feeding on scanty fare, or starving for want of food. Professor Shaler, in his " Kentucky, " ascribes to the universal walking exercise of the pioneers their lease of long life and exceptional vigor and size.

"THE ATHENS OF THE WEST."

Kentucky, a daughter of the Old Dominion, is herself old in comparison with the other States added to the Union since the Revolution. While the colonists along the Atlantic borders were resisting the tax on tea, Boone, the Columbus of the wilderness, was exploring the *new* New World beyond the Cumberland Mountains in the West. When the embattled farmers at Concord Bridge stood

> "And fired the shot heard round the world,"

the startling report, borne on the wings of rumor, came to a party of hunters encamped near the Kentucky River. They were genuine "Long Knives," dressed in buck-skin pantaloons, deer-skin leggins, a linsey hunting-shirt, bear-skin cap and moc-casins, and armed each with rifle, tomahawk, and scalping-knife, prepared to do in Kentucky as the na-tives did. By patriotic consent these rangers, one of whom was Simon Kenton, thrilled by the news of the battle of Lexington, named their encampment Lexing-ton, and four years later, in April, 1779, a village was begun near the spot. Founded but five years after Boone led the van-guard of immigration through Cum-berland Gap, and traced the old Wilderness Road through primeval solitude, Lexington is only less an-cient than a few stations like Harrodsburg and Boones-borough. The town is historically interesting, as hav-ing been a center of travel and traffic in pioneer days. It was an emporium when Cincinnati was founded, and the early Cincinnati merchants went to Lexington to buy goods.

A higher distinction belongs to this old Kentucky town. Thither, from the East, with commerce went culture. There was formed the first island of civiliza-tion in a vast savage ocean. Just outside the palisade of the absolutely necessary fort, the settlers built, with-out delay, a school-house; the stockade was a defense against Indians, the school-house a protection to knowledge and a redoubt against ignorance. John McKinney was the school-master, or, as the Anglo-Saxon word is, the "childherd," who taught the hardy flock of boys and girls who gathered in the first school-house of the West. One morning, John, waiting for his pupils, was surprised by an unexpected visit from a most unwelcome examiner, a monstrous wild-cat, which came silently in at the open door, walked across the floor and sprang at the pedagogical throat. The unarmed man of letters, after a terrific combat, killed the powerful beast by choking and crushing it upon his desk; and while its fierce teeth were locked in the flesh of his side, he said, placidly, to a rescue party who had just arrived: "Gentlemen, I have caught a cat." Theseus never performed an exploit more heroic and apposite, though he did many more mythical. The progress of civilization is well symbolized in the picture of McKinney slaying the wild-cat and then instructing the little children.

BOUQUET'S REDOUBT.
OLDEST HOUSE IN PITTSBURGH.

CHAPTER SECOND.

MASSACHUSETTS COLONIZES THE OHIO COUNTRY.

THE GREAT ORDINANCE.

Cornwallis surrendered Yorktown to Washington October 19, 1781. This surrender practically ended the Revolutionary War, but a cessation of hostilities was not proclaimed until April 19, 1783; and the peace treaty was signed, at Paris, September 3, 1783. The New Republic was born July 4, 1776. Twelve years afterwards, in 1788, the present constitution was ratified, and on April 30, 1789, the first president of the United States was inaugurated.

The Convention which formed the National Constitution first met in May, 1787. While that body was in session, the Continental Congress was holding its last meeting in New York. One of the last acts of that old Congress was to pass what is known as the "Ordinance of '87." This famous document was a set of organic laws for the government of the Territory of the United States northwest of the Ohio River. The date of its enactment is July 13, 1787. The eloquent statesman Daniel Webster said of it, in 1830: "We are accustomed to praise the law-givers of antiquity; we help to perpetuate the fame of Solon and Lycurgus; but I doubt whether one single law of any law-giver, ancient or modern, has produced effects of more distinct, marked, and lasting character than the Ordinance of 1787. We see its consequences at this moment, and we shall never cease to see them, perhaps, while the Ohio shall flow."

The Ordinance of 1787 is a document of sufficient length to cover about six printed pages of the size of this. Its first half is concerned with provisions for the temporary government of the North-western Territory, until such time as a general assembly or legislature should be organized. The duties of the governor, secretary, and judges are defined, and also the tenure of their office and the mode of appointments. A general assembly was to be formed when the number of inhabitants reached five thousand. The evils of entail and primogenture were guarded against in the provision that estates of proprietors dying intestate should be distributed among their children, or next direct heir, in equal parts. By far the most interesting and important part of the great ordinance is that comprised in the last half, or "Articles of compact between the original States and the people and States in the Territory." So vital are these "articles," and so directly significant to the millions now living in the Northwest, that they are here transcribed for convenient reference.

The Articles of Compact.

It is hereby ordained and declared by the authority aforesaid, That the following articles shall be considered as articles of compact between the original States and the people and the States in the said Territory, and forever remain unalterable unless by common consent, to-wit:

"Article 1. No person demeaning himself in a peaceable and orderly manner shall ever be molested on account of his mode of worship or religious sentiments in the said Territory.

"Article 2. The inhabitants of said Territory shall always be entitled to the benefits of the writ of *habeas corpus* and of trial by jury; of a proportionate representation of the people in the

THE PIONEER.

legislature, and of judicial proceedings according to the courts of the common law. All persons shall be bailable except for capital offenses, where the proof shall be evident or the presumption great. All fines shall be moderate, and no unusual or cruel punishment shall be inflicted. No man shall be deprived of his liberty or property but by the judgment of his peers, or the law of the land; and should the public exigencies make it necessary, for the common preservation, to take away any person's property, or to demand his particular service, full compensation shall be made for the same; and in the just preservation of rights and property it is understood and declared that no law ought ever be made, or have force in the said Territory, that shall in any manner whatever interfere with or affect private contracts or engagements, bona fide, and without fraud, previously formed.

"Article 3. Religion, morality, and knowledge being necessary to good government and the happiness of mankind, schools and the means of education shall forever be encouraged. The utmost good faith shall always be observed towards the Indians; their lands and property shall never be taken from them without their consent; and in their property, rights, and liberty they shall never be invaded or disturbed, unless in just and lawful wars, authorized by Congress; but laws founded in justice and humanity, shall, from time to time, be made for preventing wrong being done to them, and for preserving peace and friendship with them.

"Article 4. The said Territory, and the States which may be formed therein, shall forever remain a part of this confederacy of the United States of America, subject to the articles of confederation, and to such alterations therein as shall be constitutionally made, and to all the acts and ordinances of the United States in Congress assembled, conformable thereto. The inhabitants and settlers in said Territory shall be subject to pay a part of the Federal debts, contracted or to be contracted, and a proportional part of the expenses of government, to be apportioned on them by Congress, according to the same common rule and measure by which the apportionments thereof shall be made on the other States; and the taxes for paying their proportion shall be laid and levied by the authority and direction of the legislatures of the district or districts, or new States, as in the original States, within the time agreed upon by the United States in Congress assembled. The legislatures of those districts or new States shall never interfere with the primary disposal of the soil by the United States in Congress assembled, nor with any regulation Congress may find necessary for securing the title to such soil to bona fide purchasers. No tax shall be imposed on lands, the property of the United States; and in no case shall non-resident proprietors be taxed h'gher than residents. The navigable waters leading into the Mississippi and St. Lawrence, and the carrying places between the same, shall be common highways, and forever free, as well to the inhabitants of the said Territory as to the citizens of the United States, and those of any other States that may be admitted into the confederacy, without any tax, import, or duty therefor.

"ARTICLE 5. There shall be formed in the said Territory not less than three nor more than five States; and the boundaries of the States, as soon as Virginia shall alter her act of cession and consent to the same, shall become fixed and established as follows, to-wit: The western State in the said Territory shall be bounded by the Mississippi, the Ohio, and Wabash Rivers; a direct line drawn from the Wabash and Port Vincent's due north to the territorial line between the United States and Canada; and by the said territorial line to the Lake of the Woods and Mississippi. The middle State shall be bounded by the said direct line, the Wabash from Port Vincent's to the Ohio, by the Ohio, by a direct line drawn due north from the mouth of the Great Miami to the said territorial line, and by the said territorial line. The eastern State shall be bounded by the last mentioned direct line, the Ohio, Pennsylvania, and the said territorial line; provided, however, and it is further understood and declared, that the boundaries of these three States shall be subject so far to be altered that, if Congress should hereafter find it expedient, they shall have authority to form one or two States in that part of the Territory which lies north of an east and west line, drawn through the southerly bend or extreme of Lake Michigan. And whenever any of the said States shall have sixty thousand free inhabitants therein, such State shall be admitted by its delegates into the Congress of the United States, on an equal footing with the original States, in all respects whatever, and shall be at liberty to form a permanent constitution and State government; provided the constitution and government so to be formed shall be republican, and in conformity to the principles contained in these articles; and so far as it can be consistent with the general interest of the confederacy, such admission shall be allowed at an earlier period and when there may be a less number of free inhabitants in the State than sixty thousand.

"ARTICLE 6. There shall be neither slavery nor involuntary servitude in the said Territory otherwise than in the punishment of crimes, whereof the party shall have been duly convicted; provided, always, that any person escaping into the same from whom labor or service is lawfully claimed in any one of the original States, such fugitive may be lawfully reclaimed, and conveyed to the person claiming his or her labor or service as aforesaid."

REV. MANASSEH CUTLER.

The members of Congress who voted for the ordinance on July 13, 1787, were as follow: Massachusetts, Holten and Dane; New York, Smith, Harring, Yates; New Jersey, Clark and Scheurman; Delaware, Kearney and Mitchell; Virginia, Grayson, Lee, and Carrington; North Carolina, Blount and Hawkins; South Carolina, Kean and Huger; Georgia, Few and Pierce—eighteen in all. Of these the Virginia members, and Dane, of Massachusetts, were perhaps the most prominent. There has been much discussion concerning the authorship of various sections of the ordinance. Webster claimed that the part prohibiting slavery was framed by Nathan Dane. The same has been claimed for Thomas Jefferson, Rufus King, William Grayson, and Richard Henry Lee. It is certain that Rev. Manasseh Cutler had much to do with the composition as well as the adoption of the great instrument, and, although not a member of the Congress, he was invited by the committee who had the ordinance in charge, to appear before them and give the benefit of his advice, which he did. Indeed, Cutler has been called the "Father of the Ordinance of '87."

THE ORDINANCE OF EIGHTY-SEVEN.

Poem read before the Ohio Teachers' Association, at Akron, O., June 29, 1887.

I.

As a mighty heart in a giant's breast,
　　With rhythmic beat,
　　Sends marching from brain to feet
　　The crimson vigor of creative blood,
So in the bosom of the brawny West,
So in the breast of the Nation,
　　Throbs the great Ordinance — a heart,
　　A vital and organic part,
　　Propelling by its strong pulsation
The unremitting stream and flood
　　Of wholesome influences that give
　　　Unto the body politic
　　　The elements and virtues quick
　　Whereby States nobly live.

II.

Thanks to the law creators,
　　The revolutionary sages,
Who made themselves testators,
　　Bequeathing to the ages

Perpetual wealth, unbounded
Riches to posterity, compounded
   By the multiplying years,
A fortune and a legacy prodigious.
For what are diamonds and gold
To the preciousness untold
Of human freedom, civil and religious?
Thanks to the venerable seers,
   Grander than lords baronial,
   Grander than kings—the colonial
Congressmen, who, having won
Freedom with sword and gun,
   Wrote with a ransomed pen
      A Magna Charta new,
      Not for a favored few,
   But for all men,
      Ruled and rulers too.
They wrote a later Independence Declaration,
   Outlooking to the future, far discerning:
   Their principles unfolded into powers,
   As fruit expands from flowers,
      And patriotic words that burned,
      To energy of deeds were turned,
   As furnace flames that leap and glow
Compel inert machines to go;
   To generation after generation
The Congress gave whatever, in just wars,
   With sword, or pen, or tongue,
   From tyrant force was wrung
      By our brave ancestors.

III.

A new star rose in freedom's sky
   A hundred years ago;
It gleamed on Labor's wistful eye,
   With bright, magnetic glow.
Hope and courage whispered, Go,
Ye who toil and ye who wait,
   Opportune, in starlight, lo,
Open swings the people's gate!

Beyond the mountains and under the skies
Of the wonderful West your future lies.
On the banks of the Beautiful River,
By the shores of the Lakes of the North,
There Fortune to each will deliver
His share of the teeming earth.
Jocund voices called from the dark
Hesperian solitude, saying, Hark!
Hearken, ye people; come from the East,
Come from the marge of the Ocean, come!
Here in the wilderness spread a feast;
This is the poor man's welcome home!
Hither, with ax and plow;
(Carry the stripes and stars!)
Come with the faith and the vow
Of patriots wearing your scars
Like trophies upon the victorious breast;
Noblemen, wend to the West.

Load your rude wagon with your scanty goods,
And drive to the plentiful woods;
Your wheels as they rumble shall scare
The fleet-footed deer from the road,
And waken the sulky brown bear
In his long unmolested abode;
The red man shall gaze in dumb fear
At the wain of the strange pioneer;
His barbarous eyes vainly spell
The capital letters which tell
That the white-foot is bound
For the hunter's green ground
Where the buffaloes dwell.

To the Ohio country, move on!
Bring your brain and your brawn;
Some books of the best,
Pack into the chest;)
Bring your wives and your sons,
Your maidens and lisping ones;

Your trust in God bring,
Choose a spot by a spring:
And build you a castle—a throne—
A palace of logs—but your own!

Happy the new-born child
Nursed in the greenwood wild,
Though his cradle be only trough,
Account him well off;
For born to the purple is he—
The proud royal robe of the free.
For the latest time is the best,
And the happiest place is the West,
Here man shall establish anew
Things excellent, beautiful, true.

IV.

With no uncertain sound,
But like a silver bugle clear and loud
That echoes all the world around,
The ordinance, oh, teacher, summons thee

To thy vocation proud,
Annointed guardian of liberty.
'Tis written in the charter of the West
That Government must on the bed-rock rest
Of Freedom, brotherhood, equality—nor less
On whatso makes for righteousness
And knowledge, wherefore, teacher,
   With spirit reverential
   Receive thy high credential,
Sacred, like that bestowed on Gospel preacher.
   Go forth like one ordained and sent
   To lay the bulwarks of sure government ;
   As one to whom belongs
   The final righting of persistent wrongs ;
The spokes of evolution thou canst turn,
For what is human progress but to learn?
   His radical reformers God hath set
Amid young scholars in a teacher's chair,
   And the millennium is coming yet
By ways the Knights of Learning shall prepare,
   Whose shafts of truth are hurled
Into the dusky camp of Ignorance ;
   The shining banners of bold thought advance
   In every land unfurled,
And still the pedagogue, with prescient care,
   Conducts with faithful feet
   Along love's school paths sweet
   The meliorated children of the world.

Who shall establish firm and well
   Lincoln's ideal government
   Of the people for and by them,
   That shall serve and not belie them?
Who shall build the fabric stately,
   Grand beyond all precedent,
By the fathers planned so greatly?
   Build upon its vast foundation
Walls that will not crack or crumble?
Turrets that will never tumble ?
   Who shall build the people's Nation?

Educators, ye shall build
As the founders willed;
Informing and transforming girls and boys
With such foresight and afterthought
That they shall be completely taught
To master life with tranquil equipoise;
Endowed with mental force and moral beauty,
Prepared for social and for civic duty;
Each one a sovereign individual,
And yet a subject for the good of all.

v.

Well may five sister States rejoice
This glad memorial year,
Recounting with a grateful voice
The story of their proud career.
Ohio's conscious Stream partakes
The rapture of the Northern lakes,
And all the hills and vales between
Triumphant don their robes of green.
Five States rejoice; let every State
Of the Republic celebrate.
For unto each of them and all,
The blessings of the charter fall.
More than the fathers planned
Was in the wise, potential ordinance;
God took it in His hand,
Controlling so each gracious circumstance
That through the will of men His will was done,
And all the States were knitted into one.

What He hath joined let no man sever;
The holy Union stands forever!
And aye the ordinance, a mighty heart,
A vital and organic part,
Throbs on, propelling by its strong pulsation
The wholesome stream and steady flood
Of vigorous creative blood
To every nerve and fiber of the Nation.

THE OHIO LAND COMPANY OF MASSACHUSETTS.

Mr. William F. Poole, in an article published in the *North American Review*, in 1876, says: "The Ordinance of 1787 and the Ohio purchase were parts of one and the same transaction. The purchase would not have been made without the ordinance, and the ordinance would not have been enacted except as an essential condition of the purchase."

In the autumn of 1785, General Benjamin Tupper, authorized by Congress, went to the Ohio country as surveyor. He was prevented from prosecuting his proposed work by the hostility of the Indians; but from what he saw and heard of the West, he was enthusiastically in favor of planting settlements there at as early a date as practicable. In January, 1786, he visited General Rufus Putnam, at Rutland, Massachusetts, and the two veterans held a fireside conference, which resulted in the determination to attempt the formation of a company to purchase and colonize Western lands on the Ohio. They prepared an address, which was circulated by means of newspapers, giving information concerning the West and appointing places of meeting in the various counties of Massachusetts, for the purpose of selecting delegates for a general meeting to be held in Boston. Their joint call, or circular, begins by announcing that: "The subscribers take this method to inform all officers and soldiers who have served in the late war, and who are, by a late ordinance of the honorable Congress, to receive certain tracts of land in the Ohio country, and also all other good citizens who wish to become adventurers in that delightful region, that from personal inspection, together with other incontestable evidences, they are fully satisfied that the lands in that quarter are of a much better quality than any other known to New England people; that the climate, seasons, products, etc., are in fact equal to the most flattering accounts that have ever been published of them; that being determined to become purchasers and to prosecute a settlement in that country, and desirous of forming a general association with those who entertain the same ideas, they beg leave to propose the following plan, viz: That an association by the name of The Ohio Company be formed of all such as wish to become purchasers, etc., in that country, who reside in the Commonwealth of Massachusetts only, or to extend to the inhabitants of other States, as shall be agreed on."

This call, which bears the signature of both Putnam and Tupper, was dated January 10, 1786. Its suggestions were carried out. Delegates were selected from the several counties, as follow: Manasseh Cutler, Essex; Winthrop Sargent and John Mills, Suffolk; John Brooks and Thomas Cushing, Middlesex; Benjamin Tupper, Hampshire; Crocker Sampson, Plymouth; Rufus Putnam, Worcester; Jelaliel Woodbridge and John Patterson, Berkshire, and Abraham Williams, Barnstable. These assembled at the "Bunch of Grapes" tavern, Boston, March 1, 1786 Rufus Putnam was chosen chairman. The conference resulted in the appointment of a committee of five to draft a plan of organization for the contemplated land company, the committee consisting of Putnam, Cutler, Brooks, Sargent, and Cushing. On March 3d, the committee reported articles of agreement, which were adopted. The work of soliciting subscriptions for stock was at once begun. By March, 1787, two hundred and fifty shares had been taken. The company chose Putnam, Cutler, and General Samuel H. Parsons directors, and Parsons went to New York as agent of the directors, to negotiate the purchase of lands from Congress. Parsons returned to his home without effecting a purchase, and Cutler was employed to press the matter to a consummation. It was now that Cutler availed himself of the opportunity to present his

RUFUS PUTNAM.

views on the great ordinance, and to use his weighty influence for the speedy passage of that instrument.

The ordinance was enacted, as we have stated, on July 13th. Cutler's land purchase was completed fourteen days later, namely, on July 27, 1787. "Strange to say," writes Dr. B. A. Hinsdale, an eminent authority on all facts concerning the Northwest— "Strange to say, the land purchase was attended by more trouble than the ordinance of government; but,

July 27, Congress authorized the sale of five million
acres lying north of the Ohio, west of the seven ranges,
and east of the Scioto River, one million five hundred thousand for the Ohio Company, and 'the re-
mainder,' to quote Dr. Cutler's diary, 'for a private
speculation in which many of the principal characters
of America are concerned.' The total price agreed
upon was three and a half millions of dollars, but as
the payments were made in public securities, worth
only twelve cents on the dollar, the real price was only
eight or nine cents per acre."

The actual settlement of the Ohio country was
coincident with the establishment of a governmental
administration for the Northwestern Territory. Territorial officers were elected by Congress, October 5,
1787, as follow: Arthur St. Clair, governor; James
M. Varnum, Samuel H. Parsons, John Cleves Symmes,
judges; Winthrop Sargent, secretary. The action and
interests of the first settlers at Marietta were largely
moulded by the government established for the prospective people of the Northwest.

First English Settlement in Ohio.

The footsteps of a hundred years
  Have echoed since, o'er Braddock's Road,
Bold Putnam and the Pioneers
  Led History the way they strode.

On wild Monongahela's stream
  They launched the Mayflower of the West,
A perfect State their civic dream,
  A new New World their pilgrim quest.

When April robed the Buckeye trees,
  Muskingum's bosky shore they trod;
They pitched their tent, and to the breeze
  Flung freedom's star-flag, thanking God.

As glides the Oyo's solemn flood,
  Their generation fleeted on:
Our veins are thrilling with their blood,
  But they, the Pioneers, are gone.

Though storied tombs may not enshrine
  The dust of our illustrious sires,
Behold, where monumental shine
  Proud Marietta's votive spires.

Ohio carves and consecrates
  In her own heart their every name:
The founders of majestic States —
  Their epitaph: immortal fame.

The directors of the Ohio Company held a meeting at Bracket's tavern, Boston, November 23, 1787. They appointed General Rufus Putnam superintendent of their colony, and selected Ebenezer Sproat, Anselm Tupper, R. J. Meigs, and John Matthews surveyors of the newly purchased lands in the West. At the same meeting, a number of workmen, including carpenters, boat-builders, and blacksmiths, were employed to make suitable preparations for journeying to the Ohio Valley. Tools, wagons, and horses were procured, and, in December, the mechanics and others assembled at Danvers, Massachusetts, from which village they presently started for the Far West. They took their dreary way over the Alleghanies, and by the old Indian path, over Braddock's Road, and after about a month's journey reached the Youghiogheny at a point called Simrall's Ferry. General Putnam, with a smaller party made up of the surveyors and other leading men, left Hartford, in January, and pressed forward to the same place of rendezvous.

And now the stalwart New England boat-builders plied their sharp axes, and keen saws, and sounding hammers in the construction of that renowned craft, "The Mayflower," which was to carry these new Pilgrims to a new New World. This boat was the largest that had ever descended the Ohio. In length it was forty-five feet, and in width twelve feet; and it was capable of bearing a burden of fifty tons. The "Mayflower" was rudely but strongly built, with sides proof against the bullets of the red savages. She was placed under command of Captain Duval, a brave commander, who helped build the first ship launched on the Ohio River.

On the afternoon of April 2, 1788, the "Mayflower," accompanied by a flat-boat and several canoes, was unfastened from her moorings at Simrall's Ferry to float down the Youghiogheny to the waters of the Monongahela, and onward to the Ohio. On the morning of April 7th, the pioneers reached Kerr's Island, and at noon, the same day, they reached their destination and landed on the east bank of the Muskingum, about four hundred yards above its mouth and nearly opposite to Fort Harmar.

The little company that disembarked on the bank of the Muskingum, on April 7, 1788, numbered forty-eight souls. It was not until July 1st that they were reinforced by other colonists.

The first shelter erected on Ohio soil by the founders was a tent in which General Putnam had his office and transacted his business as superintendent. Above this tent floated the stars and stripes. On the 9th of April, the laws of the colony were read aloud by Benjamin Tupper, and a copy of these was posted on the trunk of a tree.

The mouth of the Muskingum had been chosen as a point for the location of a frontier military post by

General Richard Butler as early as 1785. Major
Doughty was instructed to build a fort. Late in 1785,
Major Doughty arrived at the mouth of the Muskingum
with a detachment of soldiers, and began to erect Fort
Harmar, a work which he completed in the spring of
the next year. The following description of Fort Harmar as it was in 1788, when the settlers arrived, is
from the pen of Alfred Mathews:

FORT HARMAR IN 1788.

"The fort stood very near the point on the western
side of the Muskingum, and upon the second terrace
above ordinary flood water. It was a regular pentagon
in shape, with bastions on each side, and its walls
enclosed but little more than three-quarters of an acre.
The main walls of defense, technically called "curtains," were each one hundred and twenty feet long,
and about twelve or fourteen feet high. They were

constructed of logs laid horizontally. The bastions were of the same height as the other walls, but, unlike them, were formed of palings or timbers set upright in the ground. Large two-story log buildings were built in the bastions for the accommodation of officers and their families, and the barracks for the troops were erected along the curtains, the roofs sloping toward the center of the enclosure. They were divided into four rooms of thirty feet each, supplied with fire-places, and were sufficient for the accommodation of a regiment of men. From the roof of the barracks building toward the Ohio River there arose a watch tower, surmounted by the flag of the United States."

The settlement begun on April 7, 1788, was not formally named until about three months old. It was at first known simply as the "Muskingum" settlement. But on the 2d of July, the day after the arrival of an accession of eighty-four colonists from the East, the directors and agents of the company met on the green banks of the Muskingum to give a name to their town and its squares. The town was christened Marietta, in honor of Marie Antoinette, Queen of France, the friend of La Fayette, and of American liberty.

We read with a smile, that our martial and classical forefathers named one of the squares of Marietta *Campus Martius*, another *Capitolium*, and a third *Cecilia;* and that they denominated the road through the covert-way *Sacra Vica*.

Two days after the stately naming of Marietta and its squares, on the Fourth of July, the twelfth anniversary since independence was declared, the fifth since the declaration of peace, and the last under the old articles of confederation (for the constitution had not yet gone into operation, and Washington was not yet President)—the people of the new settlement, some one hundred and thirty, and the soldiers from Fort Harmar, held a memorable celebration.

Judge J. M. Varnum delivered an address abounding in balanced sentences and rhetorical phrases. Anticipating the coming of His Excellency, Governor Arthur St. Clair, the orator exclaimed : "May he soon arrive! Thou gently flowing Ohio, whose surface, as conscious of thy unequaled majesty, reflecteth no images but the impending Heaven, bear him, oh! bear him safely to this anxious spot! And thou, beautiful, transparent Muskingum, swell at the moment of his approach, and reflect no objects but of pleasure and delight!"

Having thus glowingly apostrophized the absent governor, the gallant general addressed his "fair auditors" in still more ornate style : "Gentle zephyrs and fanning breezes, wafting through the air, ambrosial odors, receive you here. Hope no longer flutters upon the wings of uncertainty. . . . . Amiable in yourselves, amiable in your tender connections, you will soon add to the felicity of others, who, emulous of following your bright example, and having formed their manners upon the elegance and simplicity of the refinements of virtue, will be happy in living with you in the bosom of friendship." Such was the fashion of sentence-making in the days of yore. According to Dr. Hildreth, Judge Varnum was distinguished for his "brilliant language and thundering eloquence."

At the close of the oration a feast was served in a spacious bower, constructed on the point of land at the confluence of the Muskingum and the Ohio. From the fourteen toasts offered I select the following : "The United States," "The Congress," "His Most Christian

Majesty," "The New Federal Constitution," "Patriots and Heroes," "Captain Pipe, Chief of the Delawares," "The Amiable Partners of our Delicate Pleasures."

The soldiers at Fort Harmar had commemorated the great National day in 1786 by firing a salute of thirteen guns, "after which," wrote Sergeant Joseph Buel, in his diary, "the troops were served with extra rations of liquor, and allowed to get drunk as much as they pleased."

St. Clair reached Fort Harmar July 9th, and on the 15th he made his public entry, "at the bower, in the city of Marietta," and another grand ceremony took place. The Ordinance of 1787 was read, and appropriate words of welcome and response were spoken. The governor's address, though formal and stately, was warmed by a sincere eloquence evoked by the place and purpose of the meeting. In the course of his remarks he said: "The subduing a new country, notwithstanding its natural advantages, is alone an arduous task; a task, however, that patience and perseverance will at last surmount, and these virtues, so necessary in every situation, but peculiarly to yours, you must resolve to exercise. Neither is reducing a country from a state of nature to a state of civilization irksome as it may appear from a slight or superficial view; even very sensible pleasures attend it; the gradual progress of improvement fills the mind with delectable ideas; vast forests converted into arable fields, and cities rising from places which were lately the habitations of wild beasts, give a pleasure something like that attendant on creation. If we can form an idea of it, the imagination is ravished, and a taste communicated, of even the 'joy of God to see a happy world.'" General Rufus Putnam responded to St. Clair's speech.

The example set at Marietta of celebrating the "Glorious Fourth" was imitated in hundreds of other settlements subsequently formed in the West. When General Moses Cleveland, with a company of surveyors, arrived on the Western Reserve, on July 4, 1796, a patriotic demonstration was made, with speeches and joyful noise. Doubtless the orators of the day reminded their hearers that just twenty years had passed since John Adams wrote from Philadelphia to his wife, in Boston, that Independence Day "ought to be solemnized with pomp and parade, with shows, games, sports, guns, bells, bonfires, and illuminations from one end of the continent to the other, from this time forward, for evermore." With such warrant and exhortation, our patriotic fathers made the most of the anniversary, and "spread-eagle" eloquence was at a premium in the forensic market.

CIVIL GOVERNMENT ESTABLISHED.

Soon after the arrival of General St. Clair, Governor of the Northwestern Territory, he and the judges organized a formal government in accordance with the provisions of the Ordinance of 1787. Laws were issued, courts established, and all necessary civil regulations for the prosperity of the people went into effect. In due time other settlements were made, and counties and other subdivisions of a prospective State were determined. Emigration having once set toward the West, was rapid and incessant.

The first white people who settled on the north side of the Ohio—the "Indian side," as pioneers called it — formed institutions, social and civil, after the New England model, and strove to impress the stamp of Puritan ideas on family, school, church, and govern-

ment. Their preliminary task was to cut trees, provide
shelter, kill Indians, and plant seeds.

Carlyle, in one of his picturesque letters to Emerson, writes: "How beautiful to think of lean, tough
Yankee settlers, tough as gutta-percha, with most
occult, unsubduable fire in their belly, steering over
the Western mountains, to annihilate the jungle, and
bring bacon and corn out of it for the posterity of
Adam. The pigs in about a year eat up all the rattle-
snakes for miles around; a most judicious function on
the part of the pigs. Behind comes Jonathan with
his all-conquering plowshare—glory to him, too!"

Jonathan brought all of himself along when he
steered over the mountains; brought brain to direct
muscle, brought principles with his plow, and while
speculation was in his eye, it did not blind him to dis-
interested public duty. As Massachusetts began her
career with advantages not enjoyed in England, so
Ohio, the "Yankee State," or "New England of the
West," was organized under circumstances more
favorable than surrounded the colonists of the East.

The territory northwest of the Ohio was dedicated
to liberty without reserve—to complete liberty, civil
and religious.

The Ordinance of 1787 was a new mold, in which
were cast freer and better institutions than before had
been devised. Therefore the people of this region
escaped the blighting influence of imported crimes,
bigotries, and superstitions that afflicted the East and
the South.

No Roger Williams was condemned to banishment
from Ohio for liberty of speech; no innocent girl or
decrepit crone was scourged or slain for witchcraft; no
Quaker was hanged; no black man was doomed to

servitude in the new Canaan of promise north of the Beautiful Stream.

The Ordinance of 1787 places freedom, religion, morality, and knowledge as the corner-stones of civilization. The third article declares that " religion, morality, and knowledge being necessary to good government and the happiness of mankind, schools and means of education shall forever be encouraged." The Constitution of Ohio reiterates : " But religion, morality, and knowledge being essentially necessary to good government and the happiness of mankind, schools and means of instruction shall forever be encouraged by legislative provisions, not inconsistent with the rights of conscience."

To the practical men who built the first villages and tilled the first farms on the north side of the Ohio, this about education was not a mere flourish of words. Fulfilling to the letter the spirit of the organic law, Congress granting public lands, endowed Ohio University, at Athens, Ohio. Says a historian of the college: " It was the first example in the history of our country of an establishment and endowment of an institution of learning by the direct agency of the General Government." The honor of it belongs chiefly to Manasseh Cutler, and in the next degree to Rufus Putnam.

CHAPTER THIRD.

THE QUEEN CITY AND THE BUCKEYE STATE.

JOHN CLEVES SYMMES.

THE MIAMI PURCHASE OF JOHN CLEVES SYMMES.

The business relations of John Cleves Symmes to Major Benjamin Stites were somewhat similar to those of Rufus Putnam to Benjamin Tupper. Just as Tupper's information to Putnam, concerning the lands on the Muskingum, led to the formation of the Ohio Company, so the reports that Stites gave Symmes resulted in the purchase and settlement of the Miami country. In the spring of 1787, Major Benjamin Stites, a native of New Jersey, but then living at Redstone, now Brownsville, Pennsylvania, descended the Ohio River in a flat-boat, laden with flour and whisky, which staples he designed to dispose of at Limestone, or Maysville. At this point, or rather at Washington, Kentucky, Stites joined a party of pioneers and went in pursuit of some Indian thieves. The excursion brought the pursuers to a point opposite the mouth of the Little Miami River. The party crossed the Ohio on a rude raft, and continued to follow the trail of the Indians to the vicinity of Old Chillicothe, somewhere north of where Xenia now stands. Returning leisurely from this wild expedition, Major Stites had an excellent opportunity to notice the fertility of the Miami Valley, and the magnificence of its wooded scenery. The idea at once entered his mind that here was the garden spot of the Western wilderness—the most desirable location in which to plant a colony.

With this thought uppermost, he went to New Jersey, where he met, at Trenton, Judge John Cleves Symmes, then a member of Congress. Symmes had himself visited the Miami country in 1786 or 1787, and he was easily persuaded to undertake negotiations for a purchase. He accordingly petitioned Congress, August 29, 1787.

Congress granted the petition, and in October, 1787, Symmes secured his contract. Symmes published a pamphlet, announcing his purchase on the Miami, and stating the terms upon which lands would be sold. He collected a company of thirty colonists, and these, conveyed by eight wagons, each drawn by four horses, proceeded from New Jersey across the mountains, and arrived at Limestone, or Maysville, Kentucky, in the latter part of September. Major Stites, with a consid-

4

erable number of followers from Pennsylvania, was already at Limestone, and anxious to take possession of lands which he had contracted for in the Symmes purchase, at the mouth of the Little Miami. On the 16th of November, Major Stites, with a party of twenty-six, four of whom were women, and two boys, took boat and descended the river. They landed "a little after sunrise on the morning of the 18th of November, 1788," below the mouth of the Little Miami River, within the present limits of Columbia, now a part of the corporation of Cincinnati. According to Rev. Ezra Ferris, "After making fast the boat, they ascended the steep bank and cleared away the underbrush in the midst of a pawpaw thicket, where the women and children sat down. They next placed sentinels at a small distance from the thicket, and, having first united in a song of praise to Almighty God, upon their knees they offered thanks for the past, and prayer for future protection." Block-houses were built, and log cabins erected, for the shelter and protection of the little colony. Thus was founded the first English settlement in the Miami region. Stites named the town Columbia, a word which was associated not only with the memory of the discoverer of America, but which had also become a symbol of patriotism and the poetical title of the Union. Of this Columbia settlement, James H. Perkins wrote, in his "Western Annals," as follows: "The land at this point was so fertile, that from nine acres were raised nine hundred and sixty-three bushels of Indian corn. The Indians came to them, and though the whites answered, as Symmes says, 'in a blackguarding manner,' the savages sued for peace. One, at whom a rifle was presented, took off his cap, trailed his gun, and held out

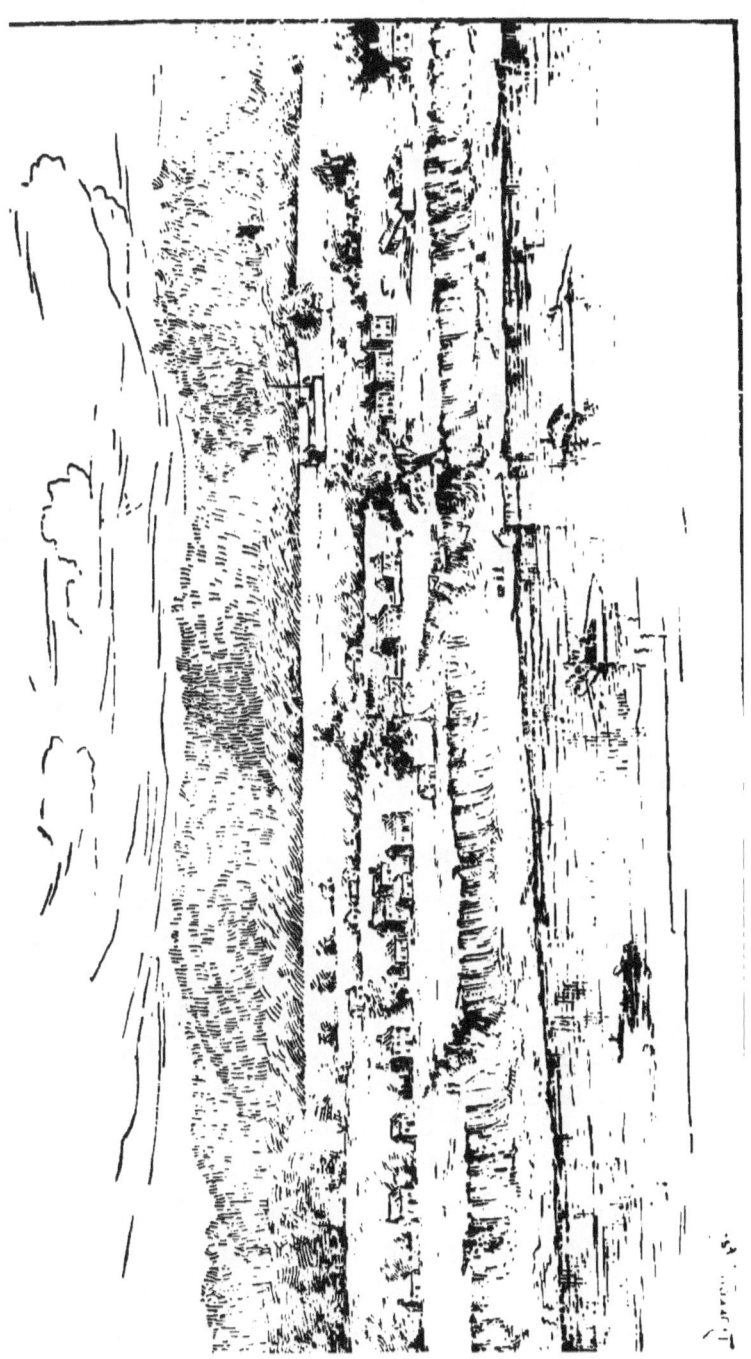

his right hand, by which pacific gesture he induced the Americans to consent to their entrance into the block-houses. In a few days this good understanding ripened into intimacy, the hunters frequently taking shelter for the night at the Indian camps; and the red men and squaws spending whole days and nights at Columbia, regaling themselves with whisky. This friendly demeanor on the part of the Indians was owing to the kind and just conduct of Symmes himself; who, during the preceding September, when examining the country about the Great Miami, had prevented some Kentuckians, who were in his company, from injuring a band of the savages that came within their power.

The Columbia settlement was, however, upon land that was under water during the high rise in January, 1789. "But one house escaped the deluge. The soldiers were driven from the ground-floor of the block-house into the loft, and from the loft into the solitary boat which the ice had spared them."

Mr. Perkins goes on to say that "This flood deserves to be commemorated in an epic; for, while it demonstrated the dangers to which the three chosen spots of all Ohio—Marietta, Columbia, and the Point—must be ever exposed, it also proved the safety, and led to the rapid settlement, of Losantiville." If the flood of 1789 deserves commemoration in an epic, what manner of poem would be adequate to describe that of 1884?

LOSANTIVILLE, OR CINCINNATI.

The story of the founding of Losantiville, or Cincinnati, the second settlement in Symmes' purchase, is full of interest.

Matthias Denman, a native of New Jersey, knowing

the projects of Symmes, took occasion to locate for himself a tract of land on the Ohio River opposite the mouth of the Licking, in January, 1788. In the following summer he visited his purchase, meditating a scheme of founding a station and establishing a ferry there. Some time afterward he was with Robert Patterson at Maysville, and later with John Filson at Lexington, and having discussed his project with them, proposed a partnership in the venture. The result of these conferences was a contract or agreement among the three parties, which is here transcribed:

A covenant and agreement, made and concluded this twenty-fifth day of August, 1788, between Matthias Denman, of Essex County, State of New Jersey, of the one part, and Robert Patterson and John Filson, of Lexington, Fayette County, Kentucky, of the other part, witnesseth: That the aforesaid Matthias Denman, having made entry of a tract of land on the northwest side of the Ohio River, opposite the mouth of the Licking River, in that district in which Judge Symmes has purchased from Congress, and being seized thereof by right of entry, to contain six hundred and forty acres, and the fractional parts that may pertain, does grant, bargain, and sell the full two-thirds thereof by an equal, undivided right, in partnership, unto the said Robert Patterson and John Filson, their heirs and assigns; and upon producing indisputable testimony of his, the said Denman's, right and title to the said premises, they, the said Patterson and Filson, shall pay the sum of twenty pounds Virginia money, to the said Denman, or his heirs or assigns, as a full remittance for moneys by him advanced in payment of said lands, every other institution, determination, and regulation respecting the laying-off of a town, and establishing a ferry at and upon the premises, to the result of the united advice and consent of the parties in covenant, as aforesaid; and by these presents the parties bind themselves, for the true performance of these covenants, to each other, in the penal sum of one thousand pounds, specie, hereunto affixing their hands and seals, the day and year above mentioned.

Signed, sealed, and delivered in the presence of

HENRY OWEN,
ABR. McCONNELL.

MATTHIAS DENMAN,
R. PATTERSON,
JOHN FILSON.

A romantic interest attaches to the name of John Filson, though his connection with the vicinity of Cincinnati is but slight. He is distinguished as being the first historian of Kentucky, and the maker of an early map of that State.

Very few copies of Filson's book and map are in existence, and the little work has been sold for as much as a hundred and twenty dollars. Next to nothing was published or generally known about Filson until quite recently, when Colonel R. T. Durret gathered together the scattered memorials of the romantic pioneer, and gave them to the world in a small volume issued by the Filson Club, Louisville. From this volume we learn that John Filson was born near Brandywine, Pennsylvania, about the year 1747, and that he came to Kentucky, probably in 1783, at the age of thirty-six. He became acquainted with, and collected information from, Daniel Boone, Levi Todd, James Harrod, Christopher Greenup, John Cowan, William Kennedy, and other pioneers. The adventures of Boone were made public by Filson, who transcribed the facts as they fell from the Colonel's lips. The first historian of Kentucky is therefore the first biographer of the famous backwoodsman. Having prepared his manuscript and map, Filson returned to the East and had them published. The next year he went from his home to Pittsburgh in a Jersey wagon ; and from Pittsburgh to the mouth of the Beargrass Creek, Kentucky, in a flat-boat. The entire journey lasted from April 25, to June 27, 1785. In the summer of the same year, he went in a canoe to Vincennes, on the Wabash, and walked back. This journey, of four hundred and fifty miles' length, he repeated in the fall, the objects of both trips being to collect material for a history of the

Illinois country. On the first of June, 1786, he set out from Vincennes in a pirogue for the Falls of the Ohio, accompanied by three men. The party were attacked by Indians, and compelled to land and take to the woods. Filson, after many dangers and sufferings, found his way back to Vincennes, almost dead from hunger and wounds. After this adventure, he traveled back to Philadelphia on horseback. In 1787, he returned again to Kentucky, and proposed to start an academy in Lexington. In August, 1788, he went into partnership with Matthias Denman and Robert Patterson in the purchase of a tract of land on the north side of the Ohio River, opposite the mouth of the Licking, on which it was proposed to lay out the town of Losantiville, now Cincinnati. Filson, who was a surveyor, marked out a road from Lexington to the mouth of the Licking, and, with his partners, arrived at their purchase in September and began to lay out the town. Before much progress had been made, Filson's life came to a mysterious end. One day he set out alone to explore the solitudes of the Miami woods, and never returned. It is supposed that he was killed by Indians. After his disappearance, his place was taken in the partnership by Israel Ludlow. It was Filson who gave to the town plat opposite the mouth of the Licking River the name LOSANTIVILLE. The street in Cincinnati now called Plum was originally Filson Avenue.

The first actual settlers of "Losantiville" were twenty-six (the same number that came to Columbia), but they were all men. Here are their names: Noah Badgeley, Samuel Blackburn, Thaddeus Bruen, Robert Caldwell, Matthew Campbell, James Carpenter, William Connell, Matthew Fowler, Thomas Gizzel (or

Gissel), Francis Hardesty, Captain Henry, Luther Kitchell, Henry Lindsey, Israel Ludlow, Elijah Martin, William McMillan, Samuel Mooney, Robert Patterson, John Porter, Evan Shelby, Joseph Thornton, Scott Traverse, Isaac Tuttle, John Vance, Sylvester White, Joel Williams.

These were of the migrating assemblage that had collected with Symmes at Maysville. They embarked on the 24th of December, 1788, probably somewhat late in the day. Strange as it may seem, the exact date of their arrival at Cincinnati has not been definitely determined. It was long held that the twenty-sixth was the time of their arrival, and that date has been celebrated as the true anniversary. But the day now generally accepted as the date of Cincinnati's founding is December 28, 1788. Their place of landing is stated to be "a little inlet at the foot of Sycamore Street, afterwards known as Yeatman's Cove." These founders of a mighty city immediately began the work of planning and building, and the town has steadily grown from that day to this.

FORT WASHINGTON.

That same suggestively-named Major Doughty, who, with his hardy command, erected the stout walls of Fort Harmar, at the mouth of the Muskingum, in 1785-86, was dispatched from that post, in August, 1789, to locate and build similar defensive works in the Miami country, within the Symmes purchase. The situation selected for the fort was a spot opposite the mouth of the Licking River, and within the town site of Losantiville. A company of seventy soldiers arrived on the ground from Fort Harmar, and the labor of building the new post was begun on or about the 20th of September, 1789—about ten months after the landing of the first settlers of Cincinnati at Yeatman's Cove. General Harmar, who for a time occupied this post as headquarters, wrote of it on January 14, 1790:

"This will be one of the most solid, substantial wooden fortresses, when finished, of any in the Western

FORT WASHINGTON.

Territory. It is built of hewn timber, a perfect square, is two stories high, with four blockhouses at the angles. . . . The plan is Major Doughty's. On account of its superior excellence, I have thought proper to honor it with the name of *Fort Washington*. The public ought to be benefited by the sale of these buildings whenever we evacuate them, although they will cost them but little."

Governor St. Clair came to Fort Washington, January 2, 1790, and, having summoned Judge Symmes, from North Bend, where the latter had planted a settlement, proceeded to issue a proclamation, erecting the

Symmes purchase into the County of Hamilton. It is generally accepted that, at the same time, St. Clair wiped out the name of Losantiville, which Filson had invented for the new ville opposite the river mouth, and substituted the name Cincinnati. No doubt the Revolutionary veteran, and trusted friend of Washington, gave this old Roman designation to the rising town out of respect to the

Society of the Cincinnati.

This society, which bore to the post-revolutionary officers of Washington's army a relation much like that which the Grand Army of the Republic bears to the Union soldiers of to-day, is thus described by Irving in his " Life of Washington :"

"Eight years of dangers and hardships, shared in common and nobly sustained, had welded their hearts together, and made it hard to rend them asunder. Prompted by such feelings, General Knox, ever noted for generous impulses, suggested as a mode of perpetuating the friendships thus formed, and keeping alive the brotherhood of the camp, the formation of a society composed of the officers of the army. The suggestion met with universal concurrence, and the hearty approbation of Washington.

" Meetings were held, at which the Baron Steuben, as senior officer, presided. A plan was drafted by a committee composed of Generals Knox, Hand, and Huntington, and Captain Shaw; and the society was organized at a meeting held on the 13th of May, at the baron's quarters in the the old Verplanck House, near Fishkill.

" By its formula, the officers of the American army, in the most solemn manner, combined themselves into one society of friends; to endure as long as they should endure, or any of their eldest male posterity, and, in failure thereof, their collateral branches who might be judged worthy of being its supporters and members. In memory of the illustrious Roman. Lucius Quintius Cincinnatus, who retired from war to the peaceful duties of the citizen, it was to be called 'The Society of the Cincinnati.' The objects proposed by it were to preserve inviolate the rights and liberties for which they had contended, to promote and cherish national honor and union between the States, to maintain brotherly kindness toward each other, and extend relief to such officers and their families as might stand in need of it.

"The society was to have an insignia called 'The Order of the Cincinnati.' It was to be a golden American eagle, bearing on its breast emblematical devices; this was to be suspended by a deep-blue ribbon, two inches wide, edged with white, significative of the union of America with France.

"Washington was chosen unanimously to officiate as president of it, until the first general meeting, to be held in May. 1784."

THE STATE OF OHIO.

The word Ohio, meaning "beautiful," is of Indian origin. In 1669, the Senecas, a tribe of the Iroquois family, told La Salle, the French explorer, "of a river which they called the 'Oyo,' or 'Oheesah,' rising in their country, and flowing to the sea, but at such a distance that its mouth could only be reached after a journey of eight or nine months." They evidently meant to describe the long water-course, including the rivers Alleghany, Ohio, and Mississippi, to which they applied the common name *Oyo*, or, sometimes, *Olygheny-sipu*, "beautiful water." As we have already related, La Salle discovered the *Oyo*, or Ohio. The country to the north of the stream came to be known as the Ohio country, or Ohio. This name was finally appropriated to designate that more limited political division, the State of Ohio.

A brief history of the organization of that State, and of its admission into the Union, is given below.

The Ordinance of 1787 provided that "so soon as there shall be five thousand free male inhabitants, of full age," in the Territory, they should "receive authority, with time and place, to elect representatives to represent them in the general assembly." The first election of territorial legislators was held Monday, December 3, 1798. The General Assembly met at Cincinnati, September 16, 1799. They selected William Henry Harrison, as delegate to the National Congress. The seat of territorial government was changed from Cincinnati to Chillicothe, May 7, 1800. On that same day the Northwestern Territory was divided by act of Congress, and Indiana Territory was created.

The ordinance says that "whenever any of the said States shall have sixty thousand free inhabitants therein, such State shall be admitted by its delegates into the Congress of the United States, on an equal footing with the original States, in all respects whatsoever; and shall be at liberty to form a permanent constitution and State government."

The Territory having acquired by 1801 a sufficient population to entitle it to secure a State government, its people petitioned Congress to pass an act to enable them to carry out the provisions of the law. Congress passed such an "enabling act" on April 30, 1802, and adjourned November 29, 1802.

Pursuant to congressional action, an election was held on the second Tuesday in October, 1802, for the election of delegates to a constitutional convention. The delegates so chosen met at Chillicothe, November 1, 1802; framed a constitution, which they adopted and signed, November 29, 1802, and immediately forwarded it to Congress. It is therefore claimed by some that Ohio became a State on November 29, 1802. But since the ratification of Congress is necessary to the formal admission of a State into the Union, many contend that Ohio did not actually become a State until February 19, 1803, on which day the National Legislature sanctioned the work of the Chillicothe convention, and recognized Ohio as a State. The State election of governor and members of the legislature was held in January, 1803, before the approval of the State Constitution by Congress and the president had been secured. The first legislature met March 1, 1803, at Chillicothe, and the government went into operation. The first governor, Edward Tiffin, was inaugurated March 3, 1803.

OHIO'S EMBLEM—THE BUCKEYE TREE.

Why is Ohio called the Buckeye State? According to Dr. S. P. Hildreth, the historian, of Marietta, the Indian traders at Fort Harmar used to distinguish Colonel Ebenezer Sproat, who was a very large man, by naming him HETUCK, or *Big Buckeye*. The application of Hetuck, or Buckeye, was extended to other white men, and finally to Ohioans in general.

Whether this be a true explanation or not, it is certain that the term *Buckeye* became attached to Ohio and its citizens at a very early period in the history of the Northwestern Territory.

A memorable celebration, in which Dr. Daniel Drake took a prominent part, was held on December 26, 1833, the forty-fifth anniversary of the settlement

WILLIAM HENRY HARRISON.

of Cincinnati. The presiding officers were: President, Major Daniel Gano; vice-presidents, William R. Morris, Henry E. Spencer, and Moses Lyon. Rev. J. B. Finley and Rev. William Burke officiated as chaplains. The character of the celebration was purely Western; those who planned it were native citizens. One hundred and sixty invited guests sat down at the

table "in the Cincinnati Commercial Exchange, on
the river bank, near where the first cabin was erected
in 1788."

The unique feature of the ceremonies was the
Buckeye Dinner, with accompanying speeches, poems,
and songs. The banquet itself was such as would
delight Mark Twain, so abundant and American it
was. Field, forest, and river contributed fruit, game,
and fish to the bounteous board. A pair of fat rac-
coons were served up smoking. The favorite potation
of the feast was called "sangaree," a sort of innocent
punch, which was dipped lavishly from four huge
bowls, carved from buckeye wood. There was also
plenty of wine, furnished by Nicholas Longworth, from
his vintage of Catawba gathered on the hills of the
Beautiful River. The formal exercises of the day con-
sisted of an oration by Mr. Joseph Longworth, a poetical address by Peyton S. Symmes, and an ode by
Charles D. Drake, of Washington, D. C. In response
to the toast, "The Emigrants, whether from the sister
States or foreign climes," Edward King presented a
poem by Mrs. Lee Hentz, in which the fair *bas bleu*
praised the "sires" who

> "First raised this city's heavenward spires,
> And based upon the unblessed sod
> The temples of the living God.
> The germs of science, genius, taste,
> They laid in the uncultured waste,
> And hallowed, with the Christian's prayer,
> The wild beasts' then untrodden lair."

There was also an after-dinner speech by the veteran General Harrison, the hero by popular favor soon
to become President of the United States.

But *the speech* of the occasion was called out by the

fifth regular toast, to "The Author of the Picture of
Cincinnati." The Doctor discoursed on the Buckeye
Tree. Happily the address has been preserved in
print, and one risks little in prophesying that it will
hold a permanent place in our literature on account of
both its subject and style. The speaker said:

"Being born in the East, I am not *quite* a native of
the Valley of the Ohio, and, therefore, am not a Buckeye by birth. Still, I might claim to be a greater
Buckeye than most of you who were born in the city,
for my Buckeyeism belongs to the *country*, a better soil
for rearing Buckeyes than the town.

"My first remembrances are of a buckeye cabin,
in the depths of a canebrake, on one of the tributary
brooks of the Licking River; for whose waters, as they
flow into the Ohio opposite our city, I feel some degree
of affection. At the date of these recollections, the
spot where we now are assembled was a beech and
buckeye grove; no doubt altogether unconscious of
its approaching fate. Thus I am a Buckeye by engraft-
ing, or rather by inoculation, being only in the bud
when I began to draw my nourishment from the
depths of a buckeye bowl.

"We are now assembled on a spot which is surrounded by vast warehouses, filled to overflowing
with the earthern and iron domestic utensils of China,
Birmingham, Sheffield, and, I should add, the great
Western manufacturing town at the head of our noble
river. The poorest and obscurest family in the land
may be, and are, in fact, adequately supplied. How
different was the condition of those early emigrants!
A journey of a thousand miles, over wild and rugged
mountains, permitted the adventurous pioneer to bring
with him little more than the Indian or the Arab car-

ried from place to place—*his wife and children.* Elegancies were unknown; even articles of pressing necessity were few in number, and when lost or broken could not be replaced. In that period of trying deprivation, to what quarter did the first settlers turn their inquiring and anxious eyes? To the buckeye! Yes, gentlemen, to the buckeye tree; and it proved a friend indeed, because in the simple and expressive language of those times, it was a friend in need. Hats were manufactured of its fibers, the tray for the delicious 'pone' and johnny-cake, the venison trencher, the noggin, the spoon, and the huge, white family bowl for mush and milk, were carved from its willing trunk; and the finest 'boughten' vessels could not have imparted a more delicious flavor, or left an impression so enduring. He who has ever been concerned in the petty brawls, the frolic and fun of a family of young Buckeyes around the great wooden bowl, overflowing with the 'milk of human kindness,' will carry the sweet remembrance to the grave.

"Thus, beyond all trees of the land, the buckeye was associated with the family circle, penetrating its privacy, facilitating its operations, and augmenting its enjoyments. Unlike many of its loftier associates, it did not bow its head and wave its arms at a haughty distance, but it might be said to have held out the *right hand of fellowship;* for of all the trees of our forest, it is the only one with five leaflets arranged on one stem—an expressive symbol of the human hand."

At another pioneer celebration, which took place December 26, 1838, the semi-centennial of the settlement of the Queen City, Doctor Drake was the orator.

5

THE BUCKEYE TREE.

When bluebirds glance the sunlit wing,
And pipe the praise of dancing spring,
Like some gay sylvan prince, and bold,
The Buckeye dons his plumes of gold.

When truants angle in the run,
Or roam the woods with dog and gun,
Young squirrels frisk and robber-bees
Maraud the honeyed Buckeye trees.

When blustering autumn dashes down
The royal forest's summer crown,
Then seek in rustling leaves to find
The Buckeye nut in bronzen rind.

My little maiden, do you know
That in the backwoods, long ago,
Fond mothers rocked their babes to rest
In Buckeye trough, like bird in nest?

Fair housewives swept their cabin rooms,
Their puncheon floors, with Buckeye brooms;
The pioneers—heaven rest their souls!
Quaffed sangaree from Buckeye bowls.

They said, the Buckeye leaves expand,
Five-fingered, as an open hand,
Of love and brotherhood the sign—
"Be welcome!   What is mine is thine!"

A century has gone, my dear,
Since those old days of pioneer,
When frontier scouts and hunters found
Our emblem tree on Western ground.

Still may the Buckeye spring and grow,
While planets roll and rivers flow!
Oh, may the Buckeye State, as long
Advance all right, oppose all wrong.

CHAPTER FOURTH.

WESTWARD BY HOOF, WHEEL, AND KEEL.

TRAVELING IN THE "DAYS OF SEVENTY-SIX."

In the year 1775, Thomas Jefferson went in his carriage, from Williamsburg, Virginia, to Philadelphia, a journey which kept him on the road ten days. So little known was the route that the distinguished traveler was twice obliged to hire a guide to keep him in the highway to the largest city on the continent. Jefferson had a coach made after a model of his own designing, and by his own workmen. It is stated, on good authority, that in the time of the Revolution there were but five coaches in New York City, and those all of English make. The importation of carriages from Great Britain was forbidden; and by the year 1786 three coach-factories were in operation in the good city of Gotham. Public stages came into use about the year 1800. The first omnibus was seen in London in 1829. Buggies were invented two or three years earlier. The heavy stage-coach of colonial days, although it made a great show of speed when dashing through a village, spent as many hours in lumbering from New York to Boston as a modern express train requires to thunder across the continent. The journey from Baltimore to Pittsburgh consumed twelve days, and was not only toilsome but also dangerous, for hostile Indians lurked in the ravines of the woods.

The indefinite region west of the Alleghany Mountains used to be styled the "Wilderness." The Rocky Mountains, or Stony Mountains, as the map named them, were known to exist, but no white man had explored them. Even within the present century the belief was held that the Missouri River had water connected with the Pacific Ocean.

Tracking Forest Paths.

In speaking of the settlement of Kentucky, we characterized' the immigrants or pioneers as a *walking* people. The Southern movers to the West were not the only pioneers who were pedestrians. The Yankees, the "Yorkers," and the Pennsylvanians learned to walk. A recent sketch in a newspaper, reporting the recollections of Mrs. Nancy Frost, who came from Pennsylvania to Marietta, Ohio, in 1789, and who was still living in January, 1887, records that the old lady remembered "some of the incidents of her journey over the mountains, and among them the fact that her mother walked most of the way, leading a cow."

Our forefathers experienced their greatest difficulties, not in navigating lake and stream, but in reaching navigable waters by untried and treacherous land routes over mountains, across unbridged rivers, and through dense, unbroken forests. The first roads in the primeval wilderness were developed on the principle of "natural selection," being the chosen paths of wild deer or bison. In the West, such rudimentary paths the hunters often called *streets* or *buffalo roads*.

TRAVELING A HUNDRED YEARS AGO.

The Indian name was "Alanantomamiowee."   Mann
Butler is my authority for recording that, in pursuing
these buffalo roads, the traveler found that "the growth
of cane was so tall and so springy as often to lift both
horse and rider off the ground, in passing over the
strong, elastic stalks."   The next phase in evolution
after these brute-made tracks was the Indian trail.
The guides that led the white man's foot toward the
setting sun were the red men, the bearers of the bow
and tomahawk.

Now the civilized ax began its sharp warfare.   The
trees were "blazed," girdled, or hewn down; and the
Indian "trail" became the white man's "trace."   It
was long before the narrow foot-ways and bridle-paths
of the woody solitude were widened into practicable
highways for wheels.

PACK-SADDLE AND SADDLE-BAGS.

First on foot, then on horse-back, came the un-
daunted pioneer.   What the canoe was to the voyager on river and lake, the pack-horse was to him who
transported merchandise by land.   Western travelers
of our own day have much to relate of the indispensable burro or mountain-donkey so much used in Col-
orado.   The pack-saddle of yore was the express car of
the back-woods, carrying passenger, freight, and mails.
Pack-horses were often driven in lines of ten and
twelve.   Each horse was tied to the tail of the one
going before, so that one driver could manage a whole
line.   The pack or burden of a single animal was of
about two hundred pounds' weight.   I have met with
the following description of the primitive pack-saddle,
by an old man whose recollection goes back to pioneer
times: "A large, forked limb was obtained, and was cut

off just below the fork, and then each was cut off about six inches from the crotch and trimmed down to the required dimensions to accommodate the loads to be carried upon it; then a flat, smooth board was strapped on the horse's back, with a sheep-skin pad under it." Mr. Speed relates an anecdote of a frontier preacher, who, at an out-of-door service, paused in the midst of his sermon to look up and point to a tree top, saying, "Brethren, there is one of the best limbs for a pack-saddle that ever grew. After meeting we will go and cut it." The art or business of making pack-saddles for sale became one of the profitable occupations of the back-woods; it is mentioned by Colonel McBride, in connection with the dressing of deer-skins for leathern breeches, as among the vanished industries.

In military operations against the Indians, pack-horse trains were the indispensable means of land transportation. Captain Robert Benham held the important position of "Conductor General" of pack-horses in the expeditions of Harmar, St. Clair, Wilkinson, and Wayne. Colonel Harmar wrote, in June, 1787, from Fort Harmar, that pack-horses could not be hired for less than fifty cents a day.

John Filson rode from his old home in Pennsylvania, to Lexington, Kentucky, on horse-back. It was no uncommon thing for men to make such long equestrian journeys. 'Twas the day of Centaurs—man and horse grew together. The saddle-bags contained the rider's rations and means of defense. The wiry steed, trained to frontier travel, climbed hills, leaped chasms, bore his master across unfordable streams. In his "Notes on the Northwestern Territory," Jacob Burnet tells that as late as 1801, on his return from the general court at Marietta, to Cincinnati, he was obliged frequently to swim his horse over streams that had neither ferries nor bridges, the Little Miami being one of these.

First Wagon Roads to the West.

Foot-paths and bridle-paths were widened by the removal of bushes and trees, and were, by slow degrees, made fit for wheels. When Braddock led his troops towards the French and Indians of Western Pennsylvania, he was obliged to cut down trees and construct a passable way through the wilderness for his wagons and ordnance. And Colonel Forbes, when he pushed his march through the woods, on his way to capture Fort Du Quesne, also improvised a practicable road. The highways thus broken were naturally made use of by the pioneer. Sections of the Braddock Road coincide with routes still traveled; other sections are abandoned, and now form part of cultivated fields. We have already described the Old Wilderness Road, by which the Virginians wended their way to the "County of Kentucky." That great Southern route of travel led through Cumberland Gap. Its counterpart was the famous Braddock Road just mentioned.

McMaster, in his chapter on "The State of America in 1784," gives a general description of the first road from the Atlantic States to the West. He says: "From Philadelphia ran out the road to what was then the Far West. Its course, after leaving the city, lay through a broken, desolate, and almost uninhabited country; now thick with towns and cities, penetrated with innumerable railways, and renowned for great deposits of iron and inexhaustible mines of coal. Thence it wound through the beautiful hills of Western Pennsylvania, and crossed the Alleghany Mount-

ains to the headwaters of the Ohio. By those, whom
pleasure or business had never led that way, it was
believed to be a turnpike. In reality it was merely
a passable road, broad and level in the lowlands,
narrow and dangerous in the passes of the mountains,
and beset with steep declivities. Yet it was the only
highway between the Mississippi River and the East,
and was constantly traveled in the summer months
by thousands of emigrants to the Western country,
and by long trains of wagons bringing the produce of
the little farms on the banks of the Ohio to the
markets of Philadelphia and Baltimore."

Oar, Rudder, and Pole.

Water-courses are Nature's routes of travel; man
finds them ready made for his use. The Mississippi,
like a great main street of the continent, was navigated,
and settlements were made on its banks long before
the interior was explored on either side. I have
already alluded to the lake travel of the French
explorers, and of the occupancy by English pioneers
of lands adjoining the lakes of New York. Passengers and goods used to be conveyed from Albany to
Schenectady—fifteen miles—in wagons; thence up the
Mohawk in batteaus of from four to ten tons' burden,
and about forty or fifty feet long, having small, movable masts. These boats were generally poled up the
stream. The process is thus described by a traveler:
"The men, after setting their poles against a rock,
bank, or bottom of the river, declining their heads
very low, place the poles against the shoulder, then
falling down upon their hands and toes, creep the
whole length of the gang-boards, and send the boat
forward with considerable speed. The first sight of

four men on each side of a boat, creeping along on
their hands and toes, apparently transfixed by a huge
pole, is no small curiosity. Nor was it until I had
observed their perseverance for two or three hundred
yards, that I became satisfied they were not playing
some pranks."

From Fort Stanwix, now Rome, goods were carried
across the country about a mile to Wood Creek, when
they were reloaded on boats and conveyed down
through Oswego Lake and River to Lake Ontario.
Further on I shall have more to say of this Northern
New York line of travel, with its wagons, portages,
and batteaus.

"TO MARIETTA ON THE OHIO."

At the close of the war for independence, migration
took a fresh start from Europe to America, and from the
Atlantic States to the West. The Ordinance of 1787
organized the Territory northwest of the Ohio River,
and the formation of the Ohio Company for Western
colonization, followed closely by the Symmes purchase,
opened the gates of travel and traffic. Ten thousand
emigrants went by the mouth of the Muskingum in
1788, seeking homes farther West. The astonishing
success of the Ohio Company in disposing of their
lands, and causing population to flow from New England to the Buckeye State, alarmed the wondering
conservatives who stayed at home. In Massachusetts,
whence General Rufus Putnam and Doctor Cutler led
their colony, it was thought, and said, and printed,
that the rush of people to the new Yankee State would
drain the old States of their best strength, and, at the
same time, ruin the fortunes of the deluded emigrants
themselves.

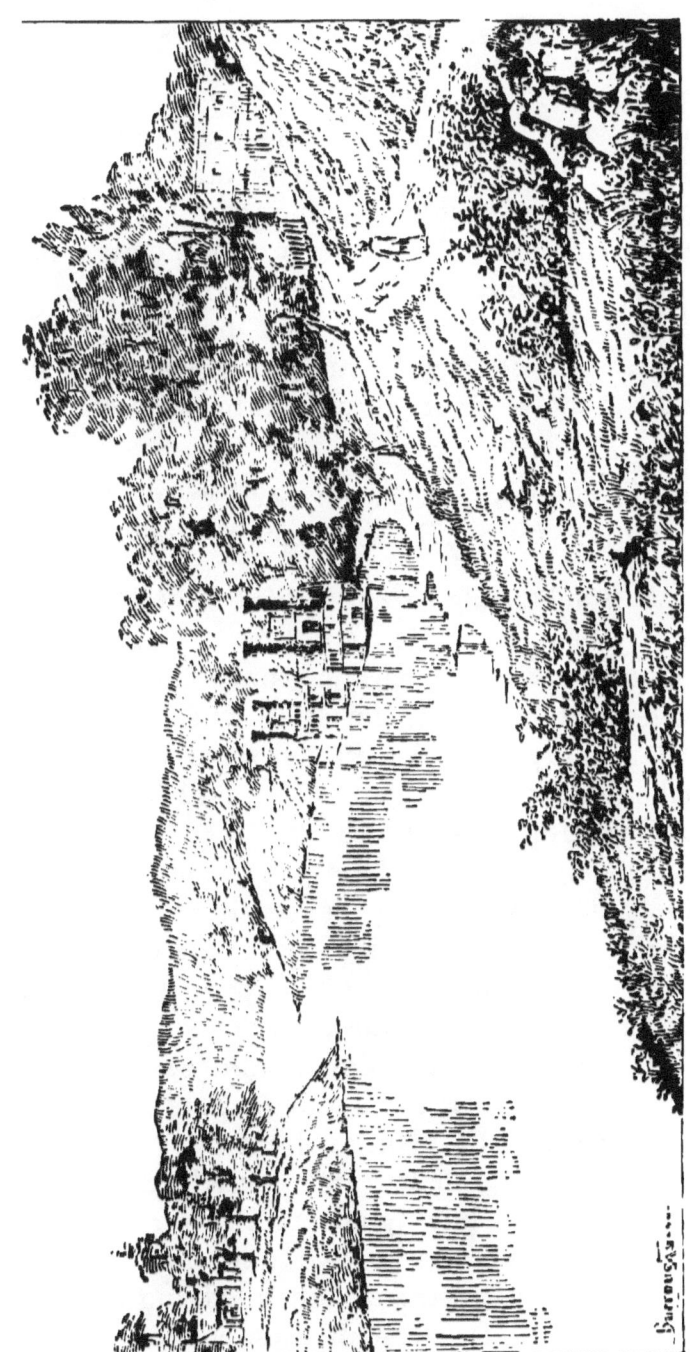

MOUTH OF THE LICKING IN 1850.

Regardless of such solemn warnings and prophecies, the movers continued to move westward to the land of promise. The Ohio Company's big, ugly wagons, with black canvas covers, showing to all eyes the large-lettered inscription, "To Marietta on the Ohio," rolled and rumbled onward over the mountains and through the valleys, bearing families and household goods, bringing axes, and spades, and guns—bringing civil arts and the moral fruits of ages into the new world.

FROM PITTSBURGH TO ST. GENEVIEVE IN 1792.—JOURNEY OF H. M. BRACKENRIDGE.

H. M. Brackenridge records his recollections of a journey by boat from Pittsburgh to St. Genevieve on the Mississippi, as early as 1792—only four years after the settlement made at Marietta—when he was not more than six years old. In ten days after starting he reached the encampment of General Wayne, at a place called Hopson's Choice, now a part of the city of Cincinnati. He beheld only a woody wilderness shut in to the water's edge, excepting the clearings made for the camp. The return voyage was made in 1795. In ascending the Ohio, the travelers frequently suffered severely from want of provisions. They met no boats going down; and excepting two log cabins at Red Bank, there were no habitations until they reached the Falls. Not far from the Wabash they saw a small herd of buffaloes and secured a large calf for their supper. Once, having encamped near a beautiful grove of sugar trees, the party found that a flock of turkeys had taken up their night's lodging over their heads. Twelve or fourteen of these served them for supper and breakfast. At another time the travelers had a "naval battle with a bear," which they attacked as he was swimming across the Ohio River. After an exciting fight, during which it for some time seemed doubtful which side would prove victorious, they dragged their valorous but vanquished foe into their boat, and he proved to be of enormous size. The fasting party encamped early in anticipation of a

OHIO RIVER FROM MT. AUBURN.

feast. "One of the paws fell to my share," says the writer of these recollections, "and, being roasted in the ashes, furnished a delicious repast."

The boat in which this journey up the river was made had a small cabin in the stern, formed by canvas stretched over hoops something like those of a covered wagon. The space beneath this was too narrow to protect more than four or five persons. The hull of the boat was entirely filled with peltries. "One night, when it rained incessantly, so many crowded in that I was fairly crowded out, and lay, until daylight, on the running-board of the boat, exposed to the falling torrents of rain, accompanied by thunder and lightning."

At the mouth of the Kaskaskia the heavy articles were removed to the rocky shore and left in charge of one man and this small child, while the proprietor and his boatmen ascended that stream for more furs. The little boy and his companion made themselves soft beds of the wild pea-plant under the spreading branches of the trees, whose vine-clad arms overhung the stream. Flocks of screaming paroquets frequently alighted over their heads, and humming birds, attracted by blossoming honey-suckle, flitted around them and flashed away again. After two days and nights spent here the boat returned, and the journey was resumed.

FROM BOSTON TO MARIETTA IN 1803.—TOUR OF REV. THADDEUS MASON HARRIS.

In the spring of 1803, Rev. Thaddeus Mason Harris made a tour from Boston to Marietta, of which he published a journal, inscribed to Hon. Rufus Putnam. Starting March 29, with a friend, he came in a private carriage, by post road, first to New York, thence through Philadelphia to Lancaster, and westward over the mountains. At Bedford the road forked; the northern branch being called the old Forbes Road, and the southern the Glade Road. The two united again twenty-eight miles from Pittsburgh. Harris took the Glade Road, which he described as very rugged and difficult, causing him to comment on the arduous enterprise of General Braddock, by whom it was cut. Braddock was a month marching one hundred miles over this road, which he made as he went along. Mr. Harris and his traveling companion were terrified by the raging fires in the mountain forests, kindled by hunters to drive out moose, deer, and other game.

At one point on the road the carriage broke down. The journey in the main was delightful, for the weather was clement, the season beautiful, and the scenery magnificent. The travelers were charmed with bird songs and wild flowers by the wayside, especially the laurel and the snowy puccoon. They lodged at inns with quaint names, such as "The Black Horse," "The Grand Turk," "The Indian Queen," finding the best accommodations at "Martins," on the Juniata, where they enjoyed neat chambers, clean beds and soft pillows, sweet water, and assiduous attention. On approaching what the tourists call the "Yokagany" or "Yok" River, they were enchanted with the lovely view.

At Wheeling they left their carriage and embarked on a keel-boat for Marietta. Multitudes of wild geese, ducks, turkeys, partridges, and quails attracted their attention, and herds of deer and other wild animals could be seen darting through the thickets. Arriving at Marietta, April 23d, Mr. Harris was entertained by General Putnam, who was living in comfort, surrounded by fruit trees of his own planting. On May 4th and 5th, Harris saw the brig "Mary Avery," the ship "Pittsburgh," and the schooners "The Dorcas and Sally" and "Amity" pass Marietta on their way to the Gulf of Mexico. The people of Marietta saluted these vessels with cheers, and salvos from a small cannon.

First Rigged Vessel Built on the Ohio.

If Doctor Harris had visited Marietta just two years earlier, he might have witnessed the launching of the first rigged vessel ever built on the Ohio. This was the *St. Clair*, which cleared from Marietta in May, 1801, and was conducted by Commodore Abraham Whipple down the Ohio and the Mississippi to New Orleans, reaching that city in July. On this occasion Captain Jonathan Devol, a citizen of Marietta, wrote an ode beginning—

> "The Triton crieth,
> 'Who cometh now from shore?'
> Neptune replieth,
> ''Tis the old commodore.'"

This same poetical Captain Devol built, in 1795, a very elegantly finished canoe, forty feet long, from the trunk of a large wild cherry tree, for carrying the mail between Marietta and the French village of Gallipolis. The boat was large enough to carry twenty men, and made a round trip once every week, being rowed by two French oarsmen.

CHAPTER FIFTH.

WESTWARD BY HOOF, WHEEL, AND KEEL.

(CONTINUED.)

FROM NEW YORK TO PITTSBURGH VIA NIAGARA FALLS.
JOURNEY OF CHRISTIAN SCHULTZ IN 1807-8.

Four or five years subsequent to Harris' tour, Mr. Christian Schultz, of New York State, a young gentleman of German origin, made what he called an inland voyage from New York City to the West and South. Schultz published a minute journal of his travels, covering a part of the years 1807-8. Going up the Hudson to Albany, he took the old route to the lakes. The freight charge from Schenectady to Utica was seventy-five cents a hundred weight, whether by water or land. The wagoners on the Schenectady Road were great rogues. From Fort Stanwix to Wood Creek a canal with locks had been constructed, so that it was no longer necessary to carry goods over the portage as formerly. In passing down Wood Creek towards Oneida Lake, the boat on which Schultz embarked met with an accident of no unusual occurrence on Western streams. A tree had fallen across the rapid current, and, despite the efforts of the boatmen, some of the boat's lading was swept overboard. From Oswego the traveler took schooner for Niagara. Visiting the Falls, he found the margin of the river on the

6

American side so obstructed by trees and bushes that it was difficult to get a view of the cataract, and he resorted to the expedient of climbing a large oak. Schultz was surprised that no public house had yet been established, but he was told that Judge P. contemplated the erection of a "genteel tavern for the accommodation of the curious." Being himself one of the curious, our enterprising tourist determined to explore Goat Island, though access to that wild paradise was difficult and dangerous. Schultz reached it safely by means of a canoe. In 1807 no road but an obscure bridle-path connected Fort Schlosser (now Niagara) with Lake Erie. Buffalo was a small village, swarming with hilarious Indians.

Crossing Lake Erie to Presque Isle, Schultz resumed his journey, going on horseback over a portage of fourteen miles to Fort Le Bœuf, leaving his baggage to be brought after him in a wagon, drawn by three yoke of oxen. The road was indescribably bad—the worst the tourist had ever seen. For a great part of the way, mire was so deep that it came up to the rider's knees as he sat in the saddle. It took from sunrise until dark of an August day to flounder fourteen miles. The ox-wagon, encountering a hidden stump, was upset, and the trunks and other baggage were baptized in mud. From Le Bœuf the journey was continued by boat down French Creek to the Alleghany, and thence to Pittsburgh. As the boat was floating down the beautiful stream, the captain shot a bear which was swimming the river, and Schultz, to his delight, shot a deer on the water's edge.

Pittsburgh is mentioned in the "Journal" as the "metropolis and emporium of this Western world." The principal business of the place was boat-building and boat-selling. Schultz bought a keel-boat for one hundred and thirty dollars, hired a crew, and acted as his own captain, floating down the Ohio to its mouth. Speculating on the prospect of future traffic between the East and the West, he concluded that New York

THE PIONEER HUNTER.

could never send any goods to the mouth of the Ohio in less than sixty days, nor at a lower rate than six dollars a hundred pounds. Harman Blennerhassett, about the same time, wrote to the "Ohio Gazette:" "It will forever remain impracticable for shipping to perform a return voyage against the currents of our great rivers."

FROM SALEM TO CINCINNATI IN 1815.—ADVENTURES
OF TIMOTHY FLINT AND HIS FAMILY.

Timothy Flint was not quite eight years old when
his uncle accompanied Putnam and the other colonists
to Marietta. Putnam started from Salem. The house
of his father, Israel Putnam, "Old Put." is still standing near the old town, and is still occupied by Put-
nams. Flint distinctly remembered, as he tells us in
the "Indian Wars of the West," the "wagon that carried out a number of adventurers from the counties of
Essex and Middlesex, in Massachusetts, on the second
emigration to the woods of the Ohio." The wagon had
a black cover, on which was painted in large white
capital letters the words, "To Marietta, on the Ohio."
It was Flint's impression that about twenty persons
accompanied this wagon, under the direction of Dr.
Manasseh Cutler.

A ray of light is thrown upon the days and ways
of yore by Flint's gossiping remark that "Dr. Cutler, at
the time of his being engaged in the speculation of
the Ohio Company's purchase, had a feud—it is not
remembered whether literary, political, or religious—
with the late learned and eccentric Dr. Bentley, of
Salem. Dr. Bentley was then chief contributor to a
paper which he afterward edited. The writer (Flint)
still remembers and can repeat doggerel verses by Dr.
Bentley upon the departure of Dr. Cutler on his first
trip to explore his purchase on the Ohio."

The departure of the emigrant wagon, the leave-
taking, and the general talk about the backwoods, kindled the imagination of young Flint. Doubtless he
felt a strong desire to join the expedition and follow
the black wagon across the mountains. Most wonder-

ful reports were spread abroad in New England concerning the inland country far toward the Mississippi. Romancing travelers told, with mock gravity, that watermelons as big as houses grew in the clearings of the West; that the flax plant in the Ohio Valley bore woven cloth on its branches; that springs of brandy and rum gushed from the fortunate hills of Kentucky. But these blessings and delights were not unmixed with evil. Stories were invented with added tenfold horror to the usual dangers of the hunt and the Indian fights; stories of storm, disease, and starvation, and of the frightful hoopsnakes, which, like a rapid wheel, span through the swamps and brakes upon its victims, its tail armed with a sting so venomous that a tree pierced ever so slightly by it instantly withered and died.

The second war with England had just closed, and the tide of migration was setting strongly toward the West, when, on October 14, 1815, Timothy Flint, with his wife and four or five children, took passage in a heavy traveling coach, bound for Pittsburgh. They started, as he had seen the emigrant wagon start nearly thirty years before, from the ancient city of Salem. Many tears were shed as the family bade their friends good-by, for, at that tine, though many went West, few came back. To the imagination the Alleghanies seemed a " barrier almost as impassable as the grave " to whomever had once crossed over.

The slow coach jostled on by the usual route, and near the end of the month began to toil over the mountains. The tavern signs, as if adapting themselves to the wild regions in which they hung, bore pictures of wolves and bears as emblems. High above the Alleghany summits the bald eagle soared. The road was difficult and dangerous. Frequently it became necessary to lift the carriage across gullies washed out by recent rains. Hundreds of "Pittsburgh wagons" were seen on the way to or from Philadelphia. Many of these had broken wheels and axles. Places were pointed out where teams had plunged down the precipice to destruction.

THE WAGONER OF THE ALLEGHANIES.

The Wagoner of the Alleghanies is a character not altogether of the past, but his tribe has diminished and his habits have changed. The poet T. B. Read has delineated in gusty rhyme one who, in anterevolutionary days, drove through the mountains that border the Juniata and the Susquehanna:

> " And even in his mildest mood
> His voice was sudden, loud and rude,
> As is the swollen mountain stream;
> He spoke as to a restive team.
> His team was of the wildest breed
> That ever tested Wagoner's skill;
> Each was a fierce, unbroken steed,
> Curbed only by his giant will;
> And every 'ostler quaked with fear
> What time his loud bells jangled near.
> On many a dangerous mountain track,
> While oft the tempest burst its wrack:
> When lightning, like his mad whip-lash,
> Whirled round the team its crooked flash,
> And horses reared in fiery fright
> When near them burst the thunder crash,
> Then heard the gale his voice of might;
> The peasant from his window gazed,
> And staring through the darkened air,
> Saw, when the sudden lightning blazed,
> The fearful vision plunging there."

This is the teamster and the team heroic! The wagoner of romantic song!

The mountain teamsters seemed to the travelers of 1815 like a new species of man. They were "unique in their appearance, language, and habits." Flint describes them as being "more rude, profane, and selfish than either sailors, boatmen, or hunters." He says: "We found them addicted to drunkenness, and very little disposed to help one another. We were told that there were honorable exceptions, and even associations, who, like the sacred band of Thebes, took a kind of oath to stand by and befriend each other." The amiable missionary adds, with a touch of pious humor, that he often dropped among them, as if by accident, that impressive tract, "The Swearer's Prayer."

Among the traveling acquaintances of the Flints were a young Connecticut printer with his pretty wife, going to Kentucky to start a "Gazette," and a burly Lutheran preacher, bound for the Big Miami, who, with pipe in mouth, rode comfortably on his horse, while his wife and young ones trudged beside their wagon.

When Flint's carriage approached the last range of the Alleghanies, the passengers, gazing out, saw a great drove of cattle and swine, which animals looked shaggy, like wolves, and the chief drover was a being as wild looking as Crusoe's man Friday. The droves were destined for the Philadelphia market, and had been driven from the valley of Mad River, in Ohio, a name which suggested to our excited travelers the idea of a savage land.

The long journey on slow wheels was at last ended, but not without the usual disaster of an upset. Just as the coach was about to enter Pittsburgh, another carriage, coming rapidly out of town, collided with it, and the next moment the Flint family were struggling and shouting under a confusion of boxes, bundles, and trunks, from which predicament they were released uninjured. Righting the vehicle, they got in again, and were soon lodged in a hotel, where the charges were double the amount asked for the same accommodations in Boston.

BOATMEN ON WESTERN RIVERS.

Flint's " Recollections " furnish an exact and vivacious account of how navigation was conducted on the Ohio and Mississippi. He says: " You hear the boatmen extolling their powers in pushing a pole, and you learn the received opinion that a ' Kentuck' is the best man at a pole and a Frenchman at the oar. A firm push of the iron-pointed pole on a fixed log is termed a ' reverend set.' You are told when you embark to bring your 'plunder' aboard, and you hear about moving ' fernent ' the stream, and you gradually become acquainted with a copious vocabulary of this sort. The manners of the boatmen are as strange as their language. Their peculiar way of life has given origin, not only to an appropriate dialect, but to new modes of enjoyment, riot, and fighting. Almost every boat, while it lies in harbor, has one or more fiddles continually scraping aboard, to which you often see the boatmen dancing. There is no wonder that the way of life which the boatmen lead—in turn extremely indolent and extremely laborious; for days together requiring little or no effort and attended with no danger, and then, on a sudden, laborious and hazardous beyond Atlantic navigation; generally plentiful as it

DOWN THE BEAUTIFUL RIVER.

respects food, and always so as it regards whisky—should prove irresistible to the young people who live near the banks of the river. The boats float by their dwellings on beautiful spring mornings, when the verdant forest, the mild, delicious temperature of the air, the delightful azure of the sky of this country, the fine bottom on the one hand and the romantic bluff on the other, the broad and smooth stream rolling calmly down the forest and floating the boat gently forward—all these circumstances harmonize in the excited youthful imagination. The boatmen are dancing to the violin on the deck of their boat. They scatter their wit among the girls on the shore who come down to the water's edge to see the pageant pass. The boat glides on until it disappears behind a point of wood. At this moment, perhaps, the bugle, with which all the boatmen are provided, strikes up its note in the distance over the waters. These scenes, and these notes echoing from the bluffs of the beautiful Ohio, have a charm for the imagination; although I have heard a thousand times repeated, is even to me always new and always delightful."

This vivid and enthusiastic description recalls the melodious lines of William O. Butler, on "The Boathorn," contributed to the "Western Review," Lexington, Kentucky, in 1821:

> "O, boatman! wind that horn again,
> For never did the listening air
> Upon its lambent bosom bear
> So wild, so soft, so sweet a strain!
> What though thy notes are sad and few.
> By every simple boatman blown,
> Yet is each pulse to nature true,
> And melody in every tone.

How oft in boyhood's joyous days,
  Unmindful of the lapsing hours,
I've loitered on my homeward way
  By mild Ohio's bank of flowers;
While some lone boatman from the deck
  Poured his soft numbers to the tide,
As if to charm from storm and wreck
  The boat where all his fortunes ride !
Delighted Nature drank the sound,
  Enchanted echo bore it round,
In whispers soft, and softer still,
  From hill to plain, and plain to hill;
Till e'en the thoughtless frolic boy,
  Elate with hope and wild with joy,
Who gamboled by the river side
  And sported with the fretting tide,
Feels something new pervade his breast,
  Change his light step, repress his jest,
Bends o'er the flood his eager ear
  To catch the sounds far off, yet dear—
Drinks the sweet draft, but knows not why
  The tear of rapture fills his eye.'

For the sake of variety, let us place beside these poetic and sentimental extracts a pen picture quite as realistic, drawn by our traveling acquaintance, Christian Schultz. For idiomatic force, local color, and sublimity of slang, literature has scarcely a match for this once famous anecdote: "On the levee at Natchez two boatmen were engaged in a drunken quarrel, incited by the charms of a Choctaw inamorata. One said, 'I am a man; I am a horse; I am a team: I can whip any man in all Kentucky, by ——!' The other replied, 'I am an alligator; half man, half horse; can whip any man on the Mississippi, by ——!' The first one again, 'I am a man; have the best horse, best dog, best gun, and handsomest wife in all Kentucky, by

——!' The other, 'I am a Mississippi snapping-turtle; have bear's claws, alligator's teeth, and the devil's tail; can whip *any* man, by——!' This was too much for the first, and at it they went like two bulls, and continued for half an hour, when the alligator was fairly vanquished by the horse."

RIVER CRAFT IN 1815.

The simplest form of floating conveyance used on the Ohio was, of course, the log canoe, or dug-out, unless we regard the raft of logs as more primitive. A larger sort of canoe, sometimes made of the trunks of two big trees united, and of a capacity sufficient to carry from ten to fifteen barrels of salt, was called a pirogue, or periogue. Who does not remember Robinson Crusoe's "very handsome periogue, big enough to hold six and twenty men?" Skiffs or batteaus were constructed of all sizes.

"Kentuck boats," also called "broad horns" and "arks," were strong, oblong structures, made of heavy, square timber, about fifteen feet wide, and from fifty to eighty feet long, covered with an arched roof. They carried a burden of from two hundred to four hundred barrels. Very large boats of the variety, intended for use on the Mississippi, were known as "Orleans boats." They were steered by a swing oar as long as the boat itself.

The "keel-boat" was of a light build and more graceful form—long, slender, and adapted to shallow water. It was propelled by poles, aided at times by a sail, or, in high water, pulled up stream by "bushwhacking;" that is, by catching hold of bushes and limbs of trees overhanging the river's margin.

The most peculiar vessel in use on the river in early

times was the "barge," a craft that looked as if it belonged to the sea. Barges were about the size of a small schooner, and carried a movable mast amidships, provided with square sails and topsails. The deck was high, and is described as having an "outlandish" appearance. The largest of these vessels carried as much as a hundred tons of freight. Three or four hands, besides the helmsman, were required to navigate the barge down stream, but to propel it against the current twenty or thirty men were needed.

PERILS OF RIVER NAVIGATION.

The perils that beset navigation when trade and migration began to penetrate the Ohio Valley were formidable. The streams themselves were unknown, treacherous, obstructed by rocks and "snags." The sentinel trees, that bent threatening from the shore, seemed hostile to inroading commerce, and with their savage arms they arrested the passing boats or dragged a share of the cargo into the waves. Behind the unfriendly trees the prowling red man waited and watched to kill the unwary voyager. Fleets of canoes would appear suddenly from some concealed cove, and a savage horde would attack some lone barge. The last memorable river fight between white men and Indians occurred between Marietta and Maysville, on the 23d of March, 1791. Captain William Hubbell, with eight men, three women, and eight children, was coming from Pittsburgh to Limestone (Maysville) on a flat-boat. The Indians, to the number of nearly a hundred, assailed the boat from their canoes. A fight with guns was kept up for many hours. All the white men but two—Captain Hubbell and another—were killed. The women and children were saved. One little boy, who had been told to stay in a certain place and keep still, whatever might happen, was shot in the leg. He made no cry. When his plight was discovered and he was asked why he had not called for help, the little hero said: "You told me to keep still, and I did."

The mail-boats that plied between Pittsburgh and Cincinnati from 1794 to 1798 were rendered proof against musket-balls, and were supplied with cannon, muskets, and ammunition.

The lower course of the Ohio came to be infested by gangs of outlaws, robbers, boat-wreckers, who had their rendezvous in woods or caves. Readers of the "Western Monthly Magazine" will recall a graphic account of the exploits of the notorious "Colonel Plug" in the vicinity of Fort Massac, the House of Nature, and the mouth of Cache.

THE CUMBERLAND ROAD.

For a good many years after the advent of the steamboat, the greater part of the produce of the upper country was transported down stream on flat-boats. But the fittest survives, and the unfit degenerate and perish. The helmsman of the keel-boat and barge was destined to give place to the pilot in his quaint wheel-house, and the dancing, drinking poleman was superseded by the modern deck-hand or "roustabout," with his leather mittens and cotton-hook.

The Indians vanished from the woods; "Colonel Plug" toppled from the unsteady deck of a floating whisky barrel into the Mississippi and was drowned; Mike Fink, the "Last of the Boatmen," was shot to the heart, and died in Missouri in the year 1822. At that date the steamboat had been ten years going

up and down the Ohio River. The employment of
thousands of keels on the great inland streams acceler-
ated the travel on the old highways, and called new
roads and canals into existence. With the breaking
up of the Indian power in the Northwest, new routes
of travel were opened through Ohio. The United
States Government transformed the old Braddock Road
into an excellent macadamized pike, from Cumber-

land, Maryland, to Wheel-
ing, West Virginia. This
great avenue of commerce,
called the National or Fed-

THE STAGE-COACH.

eral Road, was extended by State legislation through
Ohio and Indiana. Hundreds and thousands of emigrants journeyed over this road to what was still called
"The Wilderness." The heavy Conestoga covered
wagon, drawn by four or six horses, with bells, was as
picturesque an object as the barge, and was poetically
described as a mountain ship. The procession of vehi-
cles was interminable. The taverns by the wayside
were crowded, and every night movers encamped like

gypsies or like an army of peace wherever the day's
march ended.   Then came the emigrant:

> "Over the mountains to this Western land,
> A journey long and slow and perilous,
> With many hardships, and the homesick look
> Of wife and children backwards; chose his farm,
> Builded his house, and cleared, by slow degrees,
> Acres that years ago were meadows broad.
> Or wheat fields rocking in the summer heat."—*Piatt.*

The Flood of Migration in 1836.—Routes of Western Travel.

Rapidly as the torrent of population poured over
the mountains and spread into Ohio, Kentucky, Indiana and Illinois, it was long before the people of the
East realized what was going on in these States.   William G. Eliot, writing from Boston, May 30, 1785, to a
friend in Louisville, says: "Everybody is now talk-
ing of a Western tour.   It is getting to be as common
to speak of visiting Cincinnati, Louisville, and even
St. Louis, as it was five years ago of visiting Niagara.
I know a great many who have gone this spring to the
Mississippi for the sole purpose of 'seeing the West.'
All these will return with enlarged ideas, and will dif-
fuse true notions of our land of promise."

Rev. James Freeman Clarke, in the "Western Mes-
senger" for August, 1836, gives the following vivid description of the travel and routes of that day.   He says:

"The amount of travel, east and west, over the Alleghany range is so great as to almost surpass belief.
Notwithstanding the numerous routes, all are covered;
notwithstanding the yearly additions to the number
of stages and canal-boats, all are crowded, crammed,
packed, with the migratory public.   The enormous and

thickly wedged flocks of pigeons which yearly cross the Ohio in the upper element hardly exceed the human multitude who are floated, dragged, driven, and steamed along below, and their forest resting-places, stripped of foliage and beech-nuts, and broken down by their innumerable company, afford a happy analogy to the hotels and inns, whose dinner-tables are swept clean, and whose dormitories are crammed full with the ever-swelling torrent of the traveling caravans. . . The northern route, through New York State, is very beautiful. The scenery between Utica and Schenectady, on the valley of the Mohawk, is inimitably tender—the furious cataract of Trenton the exquisite lakes; Seneca, Caiuga, and Scaneateles; the beautiful towns of Rochester, Geneva, Canandaigua, Utica; the falls at Rochester and Niagara—all make this a very interesting journey. All this, however, is too well known to need any description. After leaving Buffalo, the Western traveler may either go to Pittsburgh by land, or go to Ashtabula and cross to Wellsville; or go to Cleveland, and take the canal to Portsmouth or road to Columbus and Cincinnati; or may go through the lakes, Huron and Michigan, a most delightful passage to Chicago, and thence to Peoria and down the Illinois.

"The southern route, through Virginia, is very sublime and picturesque. You may go to Fredericksburg or Richmond, thence to Charlottesville, and from thence across the Blue Ridge to the White Sulphur Springs in Greenbrier County; thence you may go to Lexington. in Kentucky, by land or more pleasantly by the sublime scenery on the Kanawha to the Charleston Salines and Guyandotte, on the Ohio. This is rather fatiguing, but the lovely grandeur of the mountain scenery is enough to repay you for it.

7

"He who aims at uniting the greatest despatch with economy and an easy route, will go from Baltimore to Wheeling on the mail route. This road is excellent, and by this route one can go from Baltimore to Cincinnati in four or five days.

"But an invalid, or one traveling with a family, who wishes to make the journey without the least fatigue, should choose the Philadelphia Canal. This majestic work has been little spoken of, though it is one of the great curiosities of the country, and, indeed, of the world."

Thomas Corwin on The Great West.

We speak of the canoe, the pack-saddle, the Kentucky boat, the Conestoga wagon, as the writer of ancient history might tell of the coracle of the wild Briton, or the chariot of Homer's heroes. But the stumps have scarcely rotted of the trees that furnished our fathers with canoes. Our oldest roads are new. In the year 1838, just half a century after the first settlement in Ohio was made at Marietta, Thomas Corwin made a speech, in the House of Representatives of the United States, in favor of a bill making appropriations for the continuance of the Cumberland Road through Ohio, Indiana, and Illinois. In that speech the famous orator made use of these words:

"Some gentlemen, (I speak it in no spirit of pride or vain boasting), some gentlemen from the old States might learn something new to them in the history of civilization would they but visit that Western world of which they often seem to me to know so little. They might see there, in the very spot where but yesterday the wild beasts of the wilderness seized their prey by night, and made their covert lair by day, on that same spot to-day stands the common school-house, filled alike with the children of the rich and the poor, those children who are to be the future voters, officers, and statesmen of the Republic. Over that vast region, so lately red with the blood of savage war, the seed-fields of knowledge are planted, and a smiling harvest of civilization springs up, and there, too, may be seen what a Christian statesman might well admire. The schoolmaster is not alone. That holy religion, which is at last the only sure basis of permanent social or political improvement, has there its voices crying in the wilderness. Upon the almost burning embers of the war-fire, round which some barbarous chief but yesterday recounted to his listening tribe, with horrid exultation, his deeds of savage heroism, to-day is built a temple dedicated to that religion which announces 'peace on earth and good will toward men.'"

HARRISON'S HOME AT NORTH BEND.

CHAPTER SIXTH.

RAPID SETTLEMENT OF THE CENTRAL STATES.

THE SONG OF THE PIONEERS.

BY WILLIAM D. GALLAGHER.

[Written nearly fifty years ago.]

A song for the Early Times Out West,
    And our green old forest-home,
Whose pleasant memories freshly yet
    Across the bosom come :
A song for the free and gladsome life
    In those early days we led,
With a teeming soil beneath our feet,
    And a smiling Heav'n o'erhead !
Oh, the waves of life danced merrily,
    And had a joyous flow,
In the days when we were Pioneers,
    Fifty years ago !

The hunt, the shot, the glorious chase,
    The captured elk, or deer ;
The camp, the big bright fire, and then
    The rich and wholesome cheer :
The sweet sound sleep at dead of night,
    By our camp-fires blazing high—
Unbroken by the wolf's long howl,
    And the panther springing by.
Oh, merrily pass'd the time, despite
    Our wily Indian foe,
In the days when we were Pioneers,
    Fifty years ago.

WILLIAM D. GALLAGHER.

We shunn'd not labor : when 't was due
　　We wrought with right good will,
And for the homes we made for them
　　Our children bless us still.
We lived not hermit lives, but oft
　　In social converse met ;
And fires of love were kindled there,
　　That burn on warmly yet.
Oh, pleasantly the stream of life
　　Pursued its constant flow,
In the days when we were Pioneers,
　　Fifty years ago.

We felt that we were fellow-men ;
　　We felt we were a band
Sustain'd here in the wilderness
　　By Heaven's upholding hand.
And when the solemn Sabbath came,
　　Assembling in the wood,
We lifted up our hearts in prayer
　　To God the only Good.
Our temples then were earth and sky ;
　　None others did we know,
In the days when we were Pioneers,
　　Fifty years ago !

Our forest life was rough and rude,
　　And dangers closed us round ;
But here, amid the green old trees,
　　Freedom was sought and found.
Oft through our dwellings, wintry blasts
　　Would rush with shriek and moan ;
We cared not—though they were but frail,
　　We felt they were our own !
Oh, free and manly lives we led,
　　Mid verdure, or mid snow,
In the days when we were Pioneers,
　　Fifty years ago !

But now our course of life is short ;
  And as, from day to day,
We're walking on with weakening step,
  And halting by the way,
Another Land, more bright than this,
  To our dim sight appears,
And on our way to it we all
  Are moving with the years.
Yet while we linger, we may still
  Our backward glances throw,
To the days when we were Pioneers,
  Fifty years ago !

A Century's Increase of Population and Growth of Settlement.

The census of 1790 gave the population of the largest six towns in the United States as follows: Philadelphia, 40,000; New York, 30,000; Boston, 18,000; Charleston, 16,000; Baltimore, 13,000; and Salem, 8,000.

George Washington had occupied the presidential chair about six weeks when Major Doughty and his men began to build Fort Washington at Cincinnati, June, 1789. Three years later, Kentucky was admitted to the Union, and four years after that, 1796, Tennessee was admitted. Ohio became a State in 1803, and in that year Jefferson's Louisiana purchase added to the possessions of our country an extent of territory west of the Mississippi greater than all that part of the United States east of that river. When he had secured Louisiana, Jefferson took measures for its exploration. An expedition was fitted out to ascend the Missouri to its source, to cross the Rocky Mountains, and to find, if such existed, a river or rivers flowing into the Pacific.

A party of thirty men, led by Captains Lewis and

Clark, started, in May, 1804, from St. Louis, then the extreme Western outpost, as Pittsburgh was before the Revolution. The party went up the Missouri, crossed the mountains, and discovered the Columbia River, being the first white men to traverse the continent by following its water-courses, an enterprise that adventurers had been attempting ever since Columbus reached the New World.

Wayne's treaty with the Indians at Greenville, in 1795, gave security to white settlers, though the red man's power was not destroyed until after the battle of Tippecanoe, in 1811, and the war with the English and their savage allies, in 1812-15.

The population of the United States at the time of this second war with England was estimated at eight millions. Few white men had yet ventured beyond the Mississippi. There were no cities west of the Alleghanies. Buffalo had about one hundred buildings, all but three of which were burned by the British. Cincinnati had some two thousand inhabitants in 1810. St. Louis had a small floating population of Yankee traders, backwoodsmen from Kentucky and Tennessee, French Creoles, and prairie Indians. The first brick house in the settlement was built in 1813. Chicago existed as a fort and two or three dwellings, but the soldiers who garrisoned the post, and the families who dwelt in the houses, were nearly all massacred by the Indians in 1812, and the fort was destroyed by fire. In the forty years that went by from the time the colonies became independent to the end of the War of 1812, only five new States were added to the original thirteen, being an average of one in eight years. The first six years after the war saw six new States admitted, one each successive year.

Growth of the States Formed from the Northwestern Territory.

The five States formed from the territory northwest of the Ohio River were admitted into the Union as follows: Ohio, 1803; Indiana, 1816; Illinois, 1818; Michigan, 1837; Wisconsin, 1848. According to tabular statements given by Dr. B. A. Hinsdale, in his "Address on the Ordinance of 1787," the increase of population in the entire region covered by these States and the parts of Minnesota and Pennsylvania that were originally included in the Northwestern Territory, an area of 265,878 acres, has been marvelous.

POPULATION WITHIN THE LIMITS OF THE ORIGINAL NORTHWESTERN TERRITORY.

Year	Population
1800	51,006
1810	272,324
1820	972,400
1830	1,470,018
1840	2,924,728
1850	4,523,260
1860	6,926,884
1870	9,121,917
1880	11,206,667

POPULATION OF THE FIVE STATES, 1800, 1810, ETC.

YEAR	OHIO.	INDIANA	ILLINOIS	MICHIGAN	WISC'NS'N	TOTAL.	POP. OF WHOLE COUNTRY.
1800	45,365	5,641				51,006	5,308,483
1810	230,760	24,520	12,282	4,762		272,324	7,239,881
1820	581,295	147,178	55,162	8,765		972,400	9,633,822
1830	937,903	343,031	157,445	31,639		1,470,018	12,866,020
1840	1,519,467	685,866	476,183	212,267	30,945	2,924,728	17,069,453
1850	1,980,329	988,416	851,470	397,654	305,391	4,523,260	23,191,876
1860	2,339,511	1,350,428	1,711,951	749,113	775,881	6,926,884	31,443,321
1870	2,665,260	1,680,637	2,539,891	1,184,059	1,054,670	9,121,917	38,558,371
1880	3,198,062	1,978,301	3,077,870	1,636,937	1,315,497	11,206,667	50,155,783

"Go West, Young Man!"

At the close of the Revolutionary War, migration moved from the trans-Appalachian States to the valley of the Ohio. By pack-horse, by river craft, by slow wheeled wagon, the movers came to settle on claims already purchased, or to seek unsold farming lands.

GOVERNOR MORROW'S MILL, ON THE LITTLE MIAMI RIVER.

Toilsome and tedious was the journey to the wilderness; the recollections of its hardships made the hope of return fade to despair.

Untried difficulties we can face—we only half believe in them and novelty stimulates; but who wishes to repeat weary tasks and privations once painfully endured? Having cast his lot in the "Ohio Country," the emigrant felt that the "Atlantic Country" was

henceforth a sort of foreign land, albeit the place of
his birth. Rarely he made a trip back to Baltimore,
Philadelphia, New York or Boston, yet the West looked
to the East for manufactured articles, for news, books,
fashions, and (at first) even for opinions, very much
as the colonies once looked to England. Just as European colonists, English, Dutch or German, brought
their customs and hereditary traits to Virginia, New
York, and Massachusetts, so the emigrants from the
old States carried their characteristics, beliefs, habits,
and material possessions to the Western wilds, there to
be modified by new surroundings and the law of natural selection. It would be curious and instructive to
study the influence of migration on the ideas, usages,
and institutions of men. We should expect that
Daniel Boone would bring to Kentucky the ways he had
learned in his native North Carolina, and that Rufus
Putnam would carry to Marietta the imprint of his
Massachusetts training. But change of circumstances
works change of habit, and the genius of the place
slowly makes men over.

The pioneers who journeyed down the Ohio and
penetrated the woods of the interior lands repeated
many of the experiences which their fathers and
even themselves had already tried east of the mountains.

They cleared lands, built cabins, planted corn,
hunted wild game, and lived in half dread of the
scalping-knife. Every man was necessarily a scout
or a ranger. The wary settler who rode with his grist
to the lonely mill carried his gun in his hand; and
when he went to the log meeting-house to worship
God, he failed not to fetch along the same faithful
weapon.

The Pioneer's House and Home.

Emerson says every house is a quotation from the woods. The cabin of the pioneer was a very direct and simple quotation. The rude edifice was fashioned entirely of timber cut from the forest, and hewn or split into shape. The ordinary dimensions were eighteen by twenty feet. The walls were of shapely logs, the roof of oaken clapboards held in their place by weight poles; the floor was of heavy planks called puncheons, cleft from large tree-trunks and smoothed with the broad-axe. The huge chimney, built on the outside of the cabin, was of stone or of cross-sticks plastered with mud. The single strong door had a wooden latch, which could be lifted from without by a leather string passing through a small hole, and called the latch-string. This was pulled inside at nights or in times of danger, somewhat after the principle of Crusoe's ladder. The window was made by sawing out a section of a log and inserting a rude frame, over which greased paper was stretched as a substitute for glass. The cabin loft, the guest-chamber of yore, was reached by a movable ladder.

The habitation in Perry County, Indiana which Thomas Lincoln built, in 1816, is described as " merely a shed of poles, which defended the inmates on three sides from the foul weather, but left them open to its inclemency in front." In this " half-faced camp " the family lived for a whole year, and then removed to another, which the writer just quoted says " was like that of other pioneers. A few three-legged stools ; a bedstead made of poles standing between the logs in the angle of the cabin, the outside corner supported by a crotched stick driven into the ground ; the table, a huge hewed log standing on four legs; a pot, kettle, and skillet, and a few tin and pewter dishes were all the furniture. The boy Abraham Lincoln climbed at night to his bed of leaves, by a ladder of wooden pins driven into the logs."

"The Raising."

The professional architect did not bring his tracing paper and India ink to the backwoods. Nor did a contractor make his bid according to plans and specifications for the masonry, the wood-work, the plastering, and the painting.

The civilization of the pioneers had not differentiated such a thing as a carpenter, much less a plumber. The principle of coöperation prevailed, however, and every man was a Jack-at-all-trades.

When Farmer Sturdy and his good wife had selected a site for their new house and home, the neighbors were notified within a circuit of eight or ten miles to come to Sturdy's house-raising on such a Monday. Each man came with axe and handspike. Suitable logs, cut from the woods, were dragged to the building spot by oxen or horses. Strong men, with some mechanical skill, were stationed at the corners of the house to notch the logs and fit them together deftly as they were, one by one, lifted to their place.

The heavy work being done, the proprietor was left to finish as he could. No one expected pay for help at a raising. The circulating currency of these hospitable days was work for work—exchange of muscular energy. The farmers lent a hand literally.

An excellent description of the log-cabin, as it appeared in Northern Ohio about the year 1809, was given by H. B. Curtis, in an address delivered in 1885 before the Richland County Pioneer Society. Mr. Curtis says : " After a few days spent in an improvised shanty, or perhaps the interior of the covered wagon, the pioneer sets himself seriously to work in the construction of his log-cabin. Having selected his spot, the tall, straight young trees of the forest are to be felled, measured, cut, and hauled to the place; at the same time properly distributed to form the several prospective sides of the proposed structure. The 'skids' are provided upon which to run up the logs. The clapboards, rived from the cleanest white oak blocks, rough and unshaved, are made ready for the roof. Whisky, then about twenty-five cents per gallon, is laid in, and due notice is given to such neighbors as can be reached of the day appointed for the 'raising,

"When the time comes. and the forces collect together, a captain is appointed, and the men divided into. proper sections and assigned to their several duties. Four men most skillful in the use of the axe are severally assigned to each corner; these are the 'corner men,' whose duty it is to 'notch' and 'saddle'—as it were, like a dovetail—the timbers at their connection, and preserve the plumb, 'carrying up' the respective corners. Then there are the 'end men,' who, with strong arms, and the aid of pikes, force the logs up the 'skids' and deliver them to the corner men. In this way the building rises with wonderful rapidity ; the beamers for the roof logs are adjusted ; the broad clapboards laid with skill, the 'weight-poles' placed upon the successive courses, and the shell of the cabin is completed. The frolic is ended and a good supper crowns the day's work. Then follow the 'puncheon' floor, made of heavy planks split from timber and dressed on one side with an axe; the big log fire-place; the beaten clay hearth; the stick and clay chimney; the 'chinking' and 'daubing;' the paper windows, and the door with wooden latch and hinges. And so the log-cabin home is made ready, and the family moves in with as much joy and delight as may fill their hearts when, twenty years later, they enter their now stately frame or brick mansion erected on the same spot."

The above is the primitive log-cabin; but it was subject to many modifications and degrees of advanced pretensions. The cabin might be single or double, with a gangway between, covered by a common roof. It was made of hewed logs, or "scutched," which was superficial hewing made after the building was up. So, too, its elevation was suited to the condition of the family; and sometimes the corners squared or dressed down; and perchance the clapboards nailed on. when so luxurious an article as nails could be obtained, in lieu of the "weight-poles."

Governor Reynolds recorded that the floors of the first houses in Illinois were the natural earth beat solid, or the earth with puncheons in the middle of the room to cover the "potato-hole," or a complete surface of puncheons. The "potato-hole" was an important receptacle in the rude dwellings of the backwoodsman. An old gentleman of Leesburg, Highland County, Ohio, told the writer of this sketch that he remembered being deposited, with three other children, in the potato-hole of his mother's house near Leesburg during a violent storm, which blew the roof from the cabin and whirled the "long-string" clock across the room. This was in 1826.

CHAPTER SEVENTH.

LOG-CABIN LIFE IN THE VALLEY OF THE BEAUTIFUL RIVER.

"THE HOOSIER'S NEST."

The pioneer's cabin of Indiana, with its furnishings and happy family, was graphically and amusingly pictured in words by John Finley, in lines entitled "The Hoosier's Nest."

THE HOOSIER'S NEST.

I'm told, in riding somewhere West,
A stranger found a Hoosier's nest,
In other words a Buckeye cabin,
Just big enough to hold Queen Mab in.
Its situation, low, but airy,
Was on the borders of a prairie;
And fearing he might be benighted,
He hailed the house and then alighted.
The Hoosier met him at the door,
Their salutations soon were o'er.
He took the stranger's horse aside,
And to a sturdy sapling tied;
Then, having stripped the saddle off,
He fed him in a sugar-trough.

The stranger stooped to enter in,
The entrance closing with a pin;
And manifested strong desire
To sit down by the log-heap fire,
Where half a dozen hoosieroons,
With mush and milk, tin-cups and spoons,

White bread, bare feet, and dirty faces,
Seemed much inclined to keep their places;
But madam, anxious to display
Her rough but undisputed sway,
Her offspring to the ladder led,
And cuffed the youngsters up to bed.
Invited shortly to partake
Of venison, milk, and johnny-cake,
The stranger made a hearty meal,
And glances round the room would steal.
One side was lined with divers garments,
The other, spread with skins of varmints;
Dried pumpkins overhead were strung,
Where venison hams in plenty hung;
Two rifles placed above the door,
Three dogs lay stretched upon the floor—
In short, the domicile was rife
With specimens of Hoosier life.
The host, who center'd his affections
On game, and range and quarter sections,
Discoursed his weary guest for hours,
Till Somnus' all-composing powers,
Of sublunary cares bereft 'em ;
And then I came away and left 'em.

The subject is a favorite one with the Western
man. "The Cabin in the Clearing" is the title of a
volume by the Indiana poet Benjamin S. Parker. The
following is from Parker's realistic description of the
remembered pioneer home.

"And I mind the floor of puncheons
   Rudely laid on joist and sill,
And the fire-place shaped and beaten
   From the red clay on the hill ;
With the chimney standing outside,
   Like a blind man asking alms,
Wrought of sticks and clay, and fashioned
   By the builder's ready palms.

"Halfway up the flue, wide-throated,
    Does the hickory cross-tree rest,
Whence depend the pot and kettle,
    When the great fire blazes best.
Oh! smell the savory venison,
    Hear the hominy simmer low
As my Mary stirs the embers
    That were ashes long ago.

"Now that cabin in the clearing
    Is but dust, blown here and there,
Where the palpitating engines
    Breathe their darkness on the air;
Where my forests towered in beauty,
    Now a smoky village stands,
And the rows of factories cluster
    Grimly on my fertile lands."

Costume and Furniture.

The comparative newness of all the material changes called by the general name of "improvements," in the Central West, may be brought vividly to the imagination by considering how recently the site of the great city of Cincinnati was in the thick woods. Timothy Flint tells us that in 1790 (not a century ago) "twenty acres in different parts of the town were planted in corn. The grinding was done with hand mills. Flour and bacon, now in such abundance, were then imported from the older settlements. The tables were of split planks, and the dishes were of wood. The men wore hunting-shirts of domestic fabric. The dress was bound with a belt, or girdle, in which were a knife and a tomahawk. The lower part of the dress was of deer-skin, and after the Indian fashion; in fact, the dress of the backwoods people of Illinois and Missouri at the present day."

SCHOOL-MASTER ON SNOWY ROAD.

This was written in 1832, only fifty-six years ago. Another chronicler of old customs informs his readers that the early settlers of Illinois wore "mawkawsins" on their feet, and covered the head with the red skin of the prairie wolf; that buffalo hides were cut into strips for ropes and traces, and that the skins of the buffalo, bear, and elk were used for beds.

The cramped limits of the ordinary log house forbade much ceremony, by compelling the members of the family to share promiscuously in miscellaneous duties. Necessities were provided for, but amenities were not. Social life, under such circumstances, suffered many inconveniences. But families learned to accommodate their wants to their means.

For toilet purposes a small looking-glass was placed at an angle above the paste-board comb-case. The men and boys always went out into the yard to wash their faces.

Usually a spinning-wheel and a flax distaff formed part of the house furniture.

Of course the historic buckeye broom or its hickory rival kept the cabin clean; and of course the necessary rifle, with accompanying powder-horn and bullet-pouch, hung upon wooden hooks against the wall.

Light, Fire, Food, and Water.

Pine-knots, tallow candles, and lard-oil lamps furnished light. The embers in the fire-place were seldom suffered to burn out, but when the last coal chanced to expire the fire was rekindled by striking a spark from the flint into a piece of tinder. The tinder-box was to our ancestors what the match-box is to us. Sometimes, when the fire went out, a burning brand was borrowed from the hearth of a neighbor.

Bread was baked in "Dutch ovens," or "bake pans," set over beds of live coals raked upon the hearth, and meats and vegetables were boiled in pots hung by hooks upon a strong piece of green timber called the "lug-pole," which was placed across the wide chimney-flue, just above the blaze. In time the lug-pole gave place to the iron crane. There was invented also a cooking utensil of tin called a reflector, by means of which biscuits were baked.

The flesh of the deer and the wild turkey furnished a staple of food in the backwoods. Beans, pumpkin butter, and dried fruits were much used. Corn-meal was the common bread-stuff, and, mills being few, the corn was often ground by means of a pestle in a wooden mortar. Corn bread was often prepared in the form of a johnny-cake—a corruption of journey-cake—a loaf baked upon a "johnny" board, about two feet long and eight inches wide, on which the dough was spread and then exposed to the fire. In Kentucky, the slaves used to bake similar loaves on a hoe, and called them hoe-cakes.

The early settler sought to locate his cabin near a spring or a running stream. When he dug a well, the water was drawn by means of the old oaken bucket, hung by a grape-vine from the "sweep," or by a windlass.

WAR ON THE WOODS.

Food, clothing, shelter, are the undowithoutables. A venison steak in the skillet, a suit of buckskin, a hut to shed the rain, and the man is comfortable. Starting with these essentials, he sets about gaining the superfluities. He begins the aggressive struggle for power and possession.

The trees are the backwoodman's enemy, for they occupy his ground. They will not run away, like the buffalo and the Indian, so they must be hewn down and cremated.

The labor of clearing, like that of building, was lightened for each by the union of all in the war upon the woods. "Choppings," and "log-rollings," were among the toilsome pleasures of the settlers.

A small army of stalwart men, with strong muscles and sharp axes, soon cut away a regiment of trees, and let daylight upon a plot of ground large enough for a "patch" for planting corn, beans, and pumpkins. The trees were felled, their branches were lopped off, their trunks were cut into lengths of from twelve to twenty feet. Then came the log-rolling. Ox-teams and handspikes dragged and rolled the slain giants of the forest into high piles, which, when dry, were burnt to ashes. When the task of the day was ended, such games as racing, wrestling, and boxing were in order.

THE CORN-HUSKING.

By slow encroachment on the woods, the tillable fields were widened. Barns to garner the harvests rose when the necessity for them was felt.

Then the custom of holding "husking bees" prevailed in the Ohio Valley, as it had prevailed long before in the East. But the mode of conducting the husking was changed. Doctor Daniel Drake gives a vivid description of corn-husking in Kentucky about the year 1800. He says:

"When the crop was drawn in, the ears were heaped into a long pile or rick, a night fixed upon, and the neighbors notified rather than invited, for it was an affair of mutual assistance. As they assembled at night-fall, the green glass quart whisky bottle, stopped with a cob, was handed to every one, man and boy, as they arrived, to take a drink. A sufficient number to constitute a sort of quorum having arrived, two men, or more commonly two boys, constituted themselves, or were by acclamation declared, captains. They paced the rick, and estimated its contractions and expansions

SCHOOL-HOUSE.

with the eye, until they were able to fix the spot on which the end of the dividing rail should be. The choice depended on the tossing of a chip, one side of which had been spit upon. The first choice of men was decided in the same way, and in a few minutes the rick was charged upon by the rival forces. As others arrived, as soon as the owner had given each the bottle, he fell in according to the end he belonged to.

"The captains planted themselves on each side of the rail, sustained by their most active operations. Here, at the beginning, was the great contest, for it was lawful to cause the rail to slide or fall toward your own end, shortening it and lengthening the other. Before I was twelve years old, I had stood many times near the rail, either as captain or private; and although fifty years have rolled away, I have never seen a more anxious rivalry, nor a fiercer struggle. It was here I first learned that competition is the mother of cheating, falsehood, and broils. Corn might be thrown over unhusked, the rail might be pulled toward you by the hand dexterously applied underneath, your feet might push corn to the other side of the rail, your husked corn might be so short a distance as to bury up the base of the pile on the other side. If charged with any of those tricks, you of course denied it, and there the matter sometimes rested; and at other times the charge was reäffirmed, and then rebutted with 'you lie,' etc., and then a fight at the moment, or at the end, settled the question of veracity.

"The heap cut in two, the parties turn their backs upon one another, and then, making their hands keep time to a peculiar sort of tune, the chorus of voices in a still night might be heard a mile. The oft replenished whisky bottle meanwhile circulated freely, and at the close the victorious captain, mounted on the shoulders of some of the stoutest men, with the bottle in one hand and his hat in the other, was carried in triumph around the vanquished party, amidst the shouts of victory which rent the air.

"Then came the supper in which the women had

been busily employed, and which always included a pot-pie. Either before or after eating the fighting took place; and by midnight the sober were found assisting the drunken home. Such was one of my autumnal schools from the age of nine to fifteen years."

THE APPLE-CUTTING AND THE "FROLIC."

When, in the course of years, orchards yielded their annual fruitage, cider flowed from the creaking press, and was stored in the cellar for liberal potation by the winter hearth.

The old-time apple-cutting was an occasion of unbounded mirth. The middle-aged and the young of a whole neighborhood assembled at some spacious farmhouse to peel and pare great heaps of apples for drying, or make into "butter" by stewing in boiled cider.

The love-fortunes of men and maids were determined by the counting of apple-seeds; and whoever removed the entire skin of a pippin in one long ribbon, whirled the lucky streamer thrice around his head and let it fall behind him on the floor, and in the form it took a quick fancy read the monogram of his or her intended mate.

After the apples were cut, and the cider boiled, the floor was cleared for a "frolic," technically so called, and merry were the dancers and loud the songs with which our fathers and mothers regaled the flying hours. The fiddler was a man of importance, and when, after midnight, he called the "Virginia Reel," such shouting, such laughter, such clatter of hilarious feet upon the sanded puncheon floor, startled the screech-owl out of doors, and waked the baby from its sweet slumber in the sugar-trough. I will not deny that Tom Wilkins, who came to the frolic dressed in a

green hunting-shirt and deer-skin trousers, drank
something stronger than hard cider, and was bolder
than he should have been in his gallant attentions to
Susan. But let by-gones be by-gones. The apple-cutting was fifty years ago, and Tom and Susan have
danced the dance of life, and their tomb-stones are
decorous enough.

THE LUXURIES OF NATURE.

We often speak of the hardships of pioneer life, and
do not overrate them; but life has compensations, and
the woods, with all its drawbacks, has its advantages
too. Think of the lavish *natural* luxuries that the
primeval forest and the *new fields* afforded. Money was
scarce, prices were higher, and artificial luxuries were
unobtainable; but the teeming soil, the woods, the
stream, the very air, were exuberant with supplies to
satisfy man's wants. The rich mold of the " truck-
patch" needed no fertilizing; the corn, beans, pumpkins, grew like magical plants. To go fishing was to
catch all the fish you wanted. An hour in the woods
loaded the hunter with game. Wild game was a pest,
so plenty it was—armies of squirrels, innumerable
pigeons.

Nuts showered from the hickory and walnut trees,
and the boys gathered them by the bushel—by the
wagon load—to crack by the cabin hearth of winter
nights. A humming music in the air, like Ariel's
choir, told the wood-wanderer of swarming bees, and
the hollow trunk of a great tree yielded honey by the
tubful and barrel. Bee-trees were sought and robbed,
in the swarming season, much in the manner
that Irving has described. Men would climb to the
hollow in which the sweet hoard was concealed, and

smoke the bees; or else the tree was chopped down and the honey secured. If the tree stood on forbidden ground, the marauding honey-robbers bored it down in silence, with a big auger.

THE OLD, OLD STORY IN THE NEW COUNTRY.

What if the rustic went clad in home-spun! What if silken gowns were unknown to the country girls in gingham or linsey, who milked the cows and churned the cream of other days!

The boys went a-courting all the same, and the damsels in linsey were angels as white as cream, and as full of sweetness as young maples in sugar-making time. For social pastime, perhaps, the swain took his sweetheart behind him on his gallant roan, and bonnily rode they away in the twilight to the party, where no piano tinkled, but where merry games consumed the hours and hearts were lost and won. The love-smitten rustic did not buy a valentine, but wrote one with a goose-quill on coarse paper, dried the ink from the "sand-box," folded the tender missive in a quaint fashion, and sealed it with sealing-wax as red as his heart's blood, or else with a wafer as tenacious as love.

When meeting-houses were established, and on evenings of revival, the good old-fashioned preacher preached and prayed loud, and the gifted elders "exhorted" there, you may be sure, came the belles and beaux; and when the benediction was spoken, those bashful beaux lurked sheepishly about the door, with heart in mouth, ready, if courage held, each to sidle up to his favorite lass and ask to accompany her home. Perhaps Angelina (for there were coquettes in those innocent days), perhaps Angelina had encour-

aged more than one bold suitor, and. as custom always
considers two company and three "a crowd," there was
rivalry at the very church portal, and the lucky escort
might pay the penalty of his triumph by a fight with
the other fellow to-morrow, for the tender passion
makes our noble sex very tough on such occasions.

Presto! Change!

The solidity and splendor of new-sprung cities in
the West; the importation from all the countries of
the world of all inventions and thoughts, to the States
that not many generations ago were unsurveyed and
unnamed; make young regions seem like old, and
confuse our conceptions of historical sequence.   To the
European traveler it appears incredible or miraculous
that so many changes, and changes so great, could have
occurred in so brief a period. Mr. Matthew Arnold.
when he lectured in the West, spoke with wonder of
this.   After addressing a large and cultured audience
of appreciative listeners at Indianapolis, he remarked,
"What a responsive assemblage! And to think how
rapidly the city must have grown. Indianapolis!
The city of Indians! And, in fact, not a century ago,
the Indians were running about here in the woods!"

The transformation is indeed astonishing. There
are men yet living who have witnessed almost the
whole series of changes in general modes of living from
the first invasion of white men upon the Ohio woods
until now. The cities and towns, of course, from the
beginning, adopted the fashions of the older places;
but country life, more self-dependent, held longer to
its primitive modes. Look on the farms, and in the
log-cabins, for good old-fashioned ways. There still
are standing thousands of log dwelling-houses in the

Ohio Valley. True, they are not built on the earliest model, but they are essentially the cabin of the backwoods. Even the stack chimney, plastered with mud, is seen now and then. But these structures are now occupied, with few exceptions, by the poorer and less

THE MOVERS.

enterprising class. Go back fifty, forty, thirty years ago, and these Central States were thickly dotted with log houses, occupied by the best of families. Read the biography of the middle-aged and old men of to-day, and note how many of them were born in such rude and primitive houses.

THE PRIMEVAL FORESTS OF OHIO.

If asked to tell in what respect the physical aspect of Ohio and Indiana has been most altered within the range of his recollection, the "oldest inhabitant" of any given county in those States—or in Kentucky— would probably answer the greatest change is that caused by cutting away the natural forest. The Creator never planted on any other portion of His globe a forest more magnificent than that which clad the primeval hills and valleys of the Ohio basin. A pioneer poet, writing forty years ago, from the very bosom of the Miami woods, sang in noble words worthy of the impressive theme:

> " Around me here rise up majestic trees
> That centuries have nurtured ; graceful elms,
> Which interlock their limbs among the clouds;
> Dark-columned walnuts, from whose liberal store
> The nut-brown Indian maids their baskets filled
> Ere the first Pilgrims knelt on Plymouth Rock ;
> Gigantic sycamores, whose mighty arms
> Sheltered the red man in his wigwam prone,
> What time the Norseman roamed our chartless seas ;
> And towering oaks, that from the subject plain
> Sprang when the builders of the tumuli
> First disappeared."

The same hand which thus pictured the forest also chronicled the progress which destroyed the glory of the scene:

> " The glory of the woods
> Faded and fell where migratory man
> Spied out the land, and chose his new abode ;
> The quiet of the sylvan solitude
> Was broken by unusual sounds, that woke
> New echoes in its depths, as through them rushed,

With arrowy speed, careering Power, that dragged
The freighted car, along whose mighty track
The monarchs of the forest disappeared;
Where the rude cabin of the pioneer
Lay like a shadow on the grassy plain,
Or, on the wooded slope,
The trellised cottage with its crown of flowers
Appeared, and statelier mansions rose anon;
The hand of civilization touched each scene,
And changed it; even our last retreats were not
Exempt, but into far secluded haunts,
Whose natural beauty art could only mar,
The axe, the compass, and the chain were borne,
Dividing and despoiling; onward came
The multitude who people now these plains
And hills, not a calm-careering stream,
But like a rushing torrent."—*Gallagher.*